CW00589707

Yes Daddy

A Daddies Inc Novel

Lucky Moon

Keep in Touch

Thanks for stopping by!

If you want to keep in touch and receive a **FREE BOX SET** as a thank you for signing up, just head to the link here: http://eep-url.com/gYVLJ1

I'll shower with you love and affection, giving you **insider information** on my series, plus all kinds of other **treats**.

My regular newsletter goes out once a week, and contains giveaways, polls, exclusive content, and lots more fun besides.

Also, you can get in touch with me at luckymoonromance@gmail.com or find me on Facebook. I love hearing from fans!

Lucky x o x

Contents

Chapter One

ISAAC

I SAAC SPOKE AS THOUGH this was the most important business deal of his life. The truth was, every deal that Isaac Righton made was the most important deal of his life.

As he paced around his large home office, he saw himself reflected in the glass doors that ran all the way along one side of the room. The guy reflected back at him looked confident and assertive. He wore a smart business suit and thick black spectacles. Although he was over forty, he clearly looked after himself. It didn't quite compute sometimes that the guy in the reflection was actually him.

Isaac's taste for money had brought him a lot of good things in life. A Miami compound with not one but four mansions on the land. All the designer clothes he could ever want. Gadgets. Free passes to some of the most exclusive clubs across the United States. Secret handshakes and hot women.

But making money came at a cost. For years of his life, Isaac hadn't taken a single day off. He ate, slept, and breathed money. Always thinking up ways to use what he had, to make more. It was an exhausting way to live, and it could be a lonely one too. For if he stopped and looked too hard at his own reflection, he saw other things too. The gray hairs at the temples, brought about by too much stress. The wrinkles around his tired eyes. The fact that there was no-one standing there beside him.

Still, none of that mattered. Not when there were business deals to be done, and banknotes to change hands. Isaac had spent so long around money that he'd gotten to know the smell, the touch, the *taste* of it. He was never able to feel bad for long when there was money around the corner. The salve that made everything feel better.

"When should we get started on the paperwork?" he asked the guy on the other end of the phone line. The guy hadn't even agreed to the deal yet, but that was a classic business move. Speak as though the deal is already done. Make it seem as though the customer would be crazy not to commit.

Of course, the deal he was offering was a good one for both him and the client. Isaac never offered bad deals. That wasn't the way to make money long-term. The way to get rich was not to simply sell a product, but a *vision*. You didn't sell a service, but an entire fucking fantasy.

Right now, he was trying to get a customer to invest in his company's newest venture: a theme park. It was kind of a wild idea, dreamed up by his colleague Montague. His other colleague, Bastion, was generally the one that sweet-talked the new potential clients. He was a pro when it came to selling fantasies. Normally more likeable than Isaac too. Isaac often came across as a little... moody. Not on purpose. He was just impatient. Always wanting to close the deal. To get to the exciting part: the cold, hard figures — which always glittered at him like diamonds in a lump of rock.

"I'm not sure..." said the guy on the phone, wavering. "I just don't know if there are enough Littles in the world to keep an entire theme park afloat. Like I told your colleague, Bastion—"

Pah.

Isaac could clinch this deal without Bastion. Bastion had grown sloppy lately. Drinking, jerking off in his office, going to strip bars. Ever since his wife had left him, he'd turned into a bit of an asshole. At least the bastard had *been* married. And no doubt he'd marry again. Even Montague was due to marry soon, to his PA, Daisy, of all people.

Well, screw those guys. Isaac Righton had never had a woman say she wanted to be with him forever, but so what? Who needed commitment when you had a hand-built Italian bed that cost over three million dollars? *And* it was one of only two pieces like that in the world? The other, as it happened, belonged to a famous rapper. It wasn't hard to guess which bed had seen more action over the past ten years. Isaac hadn't brought a girl back to his compound once.

He looked again at his reflection, reminding himself that he could do this. Running his finger through his thick, dark hair, he took a deep breath. "Anthony, my man," he said, oozing confidence. "I'm not offering you the chance to invest in a theme park. I'm offering you the chance to invest in a dream. A dream so powerful that—"

Miaow.

What the hell?

Isaac stopped pacing, looking around for the source of that strange feline noise. There was nothing in his office as far as he could tell. The windows and doors were all closed anyway, so how was a creature meant to have gotten in here? He looked toward the glass doors, but it was so dark outside that the ocean looked black. All he could see, as ever, was his own reflection.

He rubbed his eyes. It was late. He was tired. Probably imagining things.

"A dream so powerful," he began again, "that it won't just be for Littles. It'll make people into Litt—"

Miaow.

There it was again.

A scratchy, whiny noise. Definitely not pleasant. And definitely messing with his concentration.

"Is something the matter?" asked the investor, a note of impatience in his voice.

"No," said Isaac, removing his glasses and setting them down on the table. He rubbed his eyes again. "Everything's great. As I was sayin—"

Miaooooooooow.

Seriously, this was getting beyond a joke. He was so close to clinching this deal. Now there was some idiot fucking animal hiding in his room, threatening to ruin the whole thing?

"Listen, Anthony," said Isaac. "There's a problem with the line. Can't hear you too well." Didn't feel good to lie, but the truth was just too bizarre. Didn't want a potential investor thinking he was a total crackpot. "I'm gonna have to call you back, man. Speak in ten?"

The investor gave his reluctant agreement, and Isaac knew that he'd probably already messed up. You only get one chance with these people. And to think that a mewing cat—

There was a bang at the glass door.

Isaac startled, walking over to investigate and noticing a paw-shaped smear on the glass.

"Ugh," he muttered. "What a mess."

He wasn't ashamed to admit that he was a bit of a clean freak. The sight of a paw print was enough to make him pick up his phone and tell his PA, Charlotte, to schedule an earlier appointment with his window cleaner. He unlocked the door and opened it a crack, calling out into the darkness: "Shoo!"

Suddenly, he felt something small and soft pressing against his calves. When he looked down, he saw a mangy, greaseball of a kitten.

"Nuh-uh," he said, looking down at it. "No way."

Isaac was allergic to animals. The very sight of this kitten made his nose start to itch.

"You can go back out where you came from right now, you naughty thing."

The kitten looked up at him with dark, disobedient eyes.

Miaoooooooowwwwwwwwwwowowowowow!

Isaac resisted the temptation to boot the kitten out. He wasn't exactly a fan of furry creatures, sure, but he wasn't a monster. He pushed the cat gently back outside, grimacing at the feeling of its matted fur on its hands. He grabbed his phone and sent a follow-up message to his PA.

"Call animal control first thing in the morning."

Not having a stray kitten ruin another million-dollar business deal, thank you very much.

Anyway, on the subject of that possibly-ruined business deal, it was time to kiss some serious ass.

As he was about to punch in the number of the investor he'd had to hang up on, his phone buzzed in his hands.

"Anthony?" he said, unthinking. But it wasn't Anthony.

"Isaac? Is that you?"

He recognized that voice. It was the voice of a woman in her seventies. She sounded like her nose was being pinched and her ass was clenching, both at the same time.

"Aunt Meg," he said through gritted teeth. "Why are you calling me?"

A bit rude of him to talk to her like that, but he had his reasons.

"Believe me, Isaac," she said, "I wouldn't call you unless I had to. But I felt that it was only right that I give you some news."

"News?" snarled Isaac. "What news is that? You've decided to steal something else from me? My Miami compound, maybe? My business?"

Aunt Meg tutted. "Still got that temper, I see, Isaac. Well, that's what happens when you choose a life of excess."

A life of excess? He knew what she was getting at. Aunt Meg thought he slept around. She was an old-fashioned woman and a judgmental one. The truth was, Isaac hadn't slept with anyone in a long while. Didn't have time for that. And even when he did, it was usually just a fleeting fuck. Not exactly meaningless, but definitely not meaningful. There was no law against it, though. Consensual one-night stands were perfectly moral. Way better than stringing someone along for months on end if you didn't have any real feelings for them.

"I'd take a life of excess over a life of misery any day, Aunt Meg," said Isaac pointedly.

Aunt Meg said nothing for a few moments. Isaac wondered if he'd gone too far. Granted, the woman was miserable. She'd spent her life in an unhappy marriage with a man who never told her he loved her. She'd never had any close friends and she always had a look on her face like she'd just been crying.

"I'm not calling to argue with you, Isaac," said Meg. "I'm calling to tell you that your uncle has passed away."

Shit.

The old man was a grumpy asshole, but he was still a person. And so was Aunt Meg.

"I'm so sorry, Auntie," said Isaac, softening. "When's the funeral?"

"It was yesterday," came the reply.

Isaac felt a sting in his gut. "Yesterday? You didn't think to invite me?"

"Jeffrey wanted a quiet affair. Just me and him on the ranch, with the priest, of course."

Isaac ran his fingers through his hair. "Okay. Well, I'd like to come and see you. Pay my respects."

It took all his strength to say that. He didn't want to visit Aunt Meg at all. Especially not at the ranch. The ranch that used to belong to his parents. The ranch that should have been his.

He still remembered the day she told him that she was to inherit the ranch instead of him. How pathetic he felt as he asked her to let him have it. How desperately he begged to buy it off her. And how cold she looked as she told him that he couldn't have it for all the money in the world.

"There's no need for you to visit," said Aunt Meg. "I prefer my own company."

Isaac's gaze flicked over to the framed photograph on his desk. A black and white picture of the ranch, back when his parents were running it. His mother was holding him in her arms, and there were happily grazing cattle in the background. Even though he was a baby in that picture, he'd studied the scene so often that he felt as though he remembered it.

That ranch was rightfully his.

And he wasn't giving up.

"I won't take no for an answer," he said. "I'll be there at the week-end."

"I don't think—"

Isaac didn't wait for his aunt to finish what she was saying. He hung up the phone, the blood whooshing in his ears.

Just then, he heard that sound again.

Miaaaaaaooooooow.

The stray kitten.

"Ugh," he said aloud. "Fine."

He walked into his huge kitchen, grabbed a saucer and filled it generously with milk. Then, he put it outside the door for the cat.

Curious, the kitten appeared from the shadows and sniffed the saucer. Then, hungrily, it began to lap up the milk.

"Drink that, kitty," Isaac said, "then leave me in peace. There must be a hundred people in this neighborhood looking for a pet like you. I'm afraid that I'm not one of them."

The cat looked up at him with sad eyes.

Miaow?

"Oh, for goodness sake," he said. "Fine. For one night. But don't pee on any of my stuff. Okay?"

He moved the saucer into his office, and the cat came in with it. Then, he cleaned out an old box and filled it with strips of paper from his shredder. He was always fastidious about shredding. It was important to hide exactly how many figures were in his gazillion bank accounts. You could never be too careful, even in a place as secure as this.

The cat looked at its cardboard box for a moment, then it rubbed its face against it and climbed inside. It curled up among the shredded bank statements, yawned, and fell asleep. He couldn't deny it: the little thing was cute.

"This isn't a permanent arrangement, pussy-cat," Isaac whispered. "So don't get too comfortable."

Shaking his head at how easily he caved in, he felt a surge of determination.

"Take no prisoners, Isaac," he said, punching in the investor's number.

He was going to win this deal right now. Then, he was going to take back his family ranch.

Nothing — no matter how cute it was — was going to stand in his way.

Chapter Two

PEACH

"**W**ELCOME TO DADDIES INC.!"

Peach was being given a behind-the-scenes tour of her best friend's workplace. Daisy had been working at the Daddies Inc offices for a few months now. She was PA to an incredibly wealthy man called Montague Manners. As well as being Daisy's boss, Montague was also her Daddy. And, not just that: now he was her fiancé.

Obviously, Peach was thrilled for her friend. Just a few months ago, Daisy had been living in a yucky trailer having run away from her controlling ex at the altar. Now, she was dining out at fancy restaurants every weekend, holidaying on a houseboat, and getting endless orgasms from one of the richest Daddies in Miami.

Yes, obviously, Peach was thrilled. Thrilled and just a tiny bit... jealous?

Since Peach had left her old life in Connecticut, Peach's world had felt much smaller. Of course, she still had her other best friend, Kiera, who was also on the tour right now. But even though Kiera was great, she wasn't Daisy.

Daisy had been Peach's bestie since high school. They'd let Kiera into their sacred inner circle after meeting her at an ice-cream parlor, where they'd all decided to share an XXL ice-cream sundae together. Kiera was fun, feisty, and spontaneous. She wasn't afraid to speak her mind, which Peach respected, and she was super cool.

But Daisy was sweet and sunny. Always had a good word to say about someone. She knew exactly how to cheer Peach up when she was feeling down. She knew every boy (and cartoon character!) that Peach had ever had a crush on, and they'd even made up a funny secret language together. They called their pretend language *Gigglish*, and it mainly consisted of amusing noises that made them laugh so much they could no longer communicate. For example, to say "please", you had to say, "*Ziiiiiiiip?*" in a really high-pitched voice. And to say "thank you", you had to snort like a pig.

Peach and Daisy hadn't spoken Gigglish to one another in months.

And as Peach watched Daisy breeze around the Daddies Inc. offices in her fancy pink flared dress with doves all over it, she wondered if the two of them would ever speak Gigglish to one another again.

"See that room over there?" said Daisy excitedly. "That's the board-room for Littles. We call it the board*games* room!"

Peach clutched her beloved pet Shih Tzu, Teddy, tickling his brown and white fur to keep him calm. She needn't have worried, though. Teddy seemed to be loving the tour. So far, he'd been petted by three different people and given a bowl of water from the water cooler.

Peach wasn't enjoying the tour as much as her dog. It was hard to put aside her feelings of jealousy. She looked at Kiera, wondering if she was feeling a tiny bit sad like she was, but Kiera looked genuinely into it.

"This is so awesome, Daze," said Kiera. "It's like you work at the Google headquarters or something."

Daisy smiled. "Actually, Montague took me to a meeting at the Google headquarters a couple weeks ago," she said, "and it turns out, our offices are better!"

"Now, now," said Montague, pressing a finger to his lips. "Let's not get boastful, young lady. Pride comes before a fall, remember?"

Montague had come along for the start of the tour too, and he'd been charming as ever, always knowing just how far to push the Daddy thing in public. Clearly, in a workplace like this, it was okay to be open about being in an age play relationship, but Montague was Daisy's boss, so he had to remain professional.

"Sorry, Daddy," said Daisy, stifling a smile.

Montague gave her a stern look. Then, he turned back to Peach and Kiera. "This is where I leave you, ladies," he said. "Got a meeting to prepare for. I'll leave you in Daisy's capable hands."

Daisy held up her hands, grinning, and Peach caught sight of the huge diamond and aquamarine ring she was wearing. Peach couldn't believe that Daisy was getting married so soon after running away from her last wedding. She knew that Montague was the right man for her best friend, but, but, but...

Well, it all came down to jealousy again, didn't it?

It was strange feeling like Daisy had someone else to confide in these days. Like Peach wasn't the first person she told her news to. Also, Daisy and Montague were getting married in a month, and they were keeping all the details of it a total secret, including the venue. It was one of the first secrets Daisy had ever kept from her, and she hated to admit it to herself, but it felt kinda crappy.

"Alright!" said Daisy, full of energy. "Now we can start the *real* tour!" She turned to her friends and wiggled her eyebrows.

"What do you mean?" asked Kiera. "That tour we had just then wasn't real?"

"Well, sure it was," said Daisy. "But now I can give you the gossip. Like, ooh! Look over there!"

She pointed through a large glass window that was frosted up to chest height, as though to obscure whoever might be sitting in the room having a meeting. There was someone standing in there, though, clearly visible above the frosting. It was a tall man with wide shoulders and black-rimmed spectacles. He was leading a meeting with three other men who seemed to be eating out of the palm of his hand. Behind him was a spreadsheet projected onto the wall, with some impossibly large numbers on it.

"That's Isaac," said Daisy. "He's smart with numbers. And according to Montague, he's the richest guy at Daddy's Inc."

"Oooh," said Kiera, "he's kinda dishy. Tell me more."

"Ha!" Daisy laughed. "Don't even think about it! Isaac's a man of mystery. He never shows the slightest bit of interest in anyone here, he never reveals anything about himself, he never laughs at anyone's jokes, and he's kind of a grump."

"I thought grumps were your specialty, Daisy," Kiera joked, looking away from Isaac and seeming to lose all interest in him.

As Peach looked at him, though, it was like a lightbulb was going off in her head. Not because she was attracted to him, although there definitely was something about him. He had that brains *and* brawn vibe going on that was undoubtedly intriguing. But more important than that was what he represented.

All those numbers. All that money. For so long, Peach had been afraid to let herself dream big. She'd tried to switch off the part of herself that wanted nice things and a nice life. She used to have so much ambition.

Over the years, though, she'd settled for rags over riches. She'd managed to convince herself that it was somehow virtuous to be poor.

Back in Connecticut, she volunteered at a dog rescue place two days a week, and worked part-time at a dog-grooming parlor the rest of the time. She wasn't allowed to groom the animals, though. Her job was sweeping up the clippings and washing down the tables after the dogs were treated. Her boss told her that she wasn't good enough to touch the animals, even though she groomed her own dog's hair, and he always looked marvelous.

She's always wondered if part of the reason that she wouldn't allow herself to dream big was because she was a Little. She'd always felt a bit of shame about that part of herself. It didn't help that her parents had told her not to bother contacting them until she'd "grown up". They told her that she was too childish, and needed to stop watching cartoons and wearing PAW Patrol onesies and get a proper job.

Being here — in a billion-dollar empire — where Littles were celebrated not hated — was inspiring.

"Look, Teddy," she said, holding her dog up to look at Isaac and his spreadsheet. "Do you think that could be us one day?" she whispered into his floppy little ear. "Running our own business with a bazillion dollars in the bank. Whaddya reckon?"

Teddy licked his nose, oblivious to what she was asking him, but cute all the same.

Teddy had come from the rescue center that Peach volunteered at. He'd been there for months before she adopted him, but nobody wanted him. He was blind in one eye and when he barked it sounded a bit like nails scratching down a chalkboard. But he came into Peach's life when she really needed him. Her anxiety was bad after her parents cut her out of their life. She had a stammer and hid indoors with agoraphobia some days. Teddy helped her with all that.

As Peach held Teddy up to the glass, she noticed Isaac's head turning toward her. He looked at Peach with an expression of mild interest, then he looked at Teddy with an expression of strong disgust.

"Uh oh," said Daisy. "We should probably keep moving. Isaac's not the biggest fan of—"

Peach watched Isaac stride across the room toward her, then he opened the door, pointing a finger straight at Teddy.

"No animals!" he boomed.

"Sorry, sir," said Daisy. "Montague said we were allowed to make an exception for—"

"Montague is a soft touch," he said. "People could have allergies. The dog could make a mess. It could hurt someone."

Peach lifted one of Teddy's little paws and pulled a cute expression. "I won't hurt anyone," she said in a funny little voice, pretending to be Teddy. "I'm actually hypoallergenic because *technically* Shih Tzus have hair instead of fur—"

"Did I not make myself clear?" asked Isaac. "No. Animals."

Peach sighed. Quietly, she said, "We're all animals, you know."

"Get the mutt outside," Isaac instructed Peach. "And Daisy? Tell my PA to cancel my meetings on Saturday. I'm heading back to my ranch."

"I didn't know you had a ranch, sir," said Daisy.

"I don't," replied Isaac. "Yet." He went back into his office, slamming the door.

Peach looked at Daisy. "Do we really have to go?"

Daisy grimaced. "Yeah. Sorry. But don't worry. Kiera and I will catch up with you later."

"Wait," said Peach. "You're going to keep running the tour without me?"

"Just for an hour or so," said Daisy. "It'll fly by. Promise."

And with that, both of Peach's friends were gone.

Chapter Three

ISAAC

I SAAC SLAMMED ON THE brakes of his Rolls-Royce SUV. This was the ranch, but it was not the ranch that he remembered.

For a start, the perimeter that his dad had worked so hard to build was falling down. Not that it really mattered, because there were only half a dozen cattle remaining on the land, and they all looked so scrawny and weak that they were clearly going nowhere in a hurry. He'd have liked to have gone to take a closer look at them, but unfortunately, his allergies would have played up. His allergies were never really an issue when he was a kid, but after all his years in the city, he could hardly go near anything with fur.

He looked over at the ranch house. Two of its windows were boarded up, it needed its guttering fixing, and there was a pile of trash on one side of the driveway that looked so old and so rusted it had clearly been there for years.

"Jeez," Isaac muttered to himself as he got out of the vehicle.

How had Aunt Meg let it get like this? This place had obviously been run into the ground over a period of years, long before Uncle Jeffrey died.

Isaac walked up to the house with a sense of trepidation. This was the home that he'd grown up in. He'd been born on the kitchen floor

— a story that his mother had always loved to tell whenever they had guests around.

"Did you know," she used to say, "that my sweet little Isey was born on the very spot you're now eating your dinner?"

Isaac shivered at the memory. Such happy times. So much had changed since those days.

Eying the front door with distaste, he knocked. Attached to the front door was a gaudy plaque that read: "Welcome — ish. Depends on who you are and how long you stay." Under that, there was a handwritten note that said: "No junk, no bills, no dicks."

Well. This was going to be fun...

Isaac waited a while, then knocked again. "Aunt Meg!" he called. "It's Isaac."

Eventually, he heard shuffling behind the door and his aunt opened it a crack, still leaving it on the latch.

She peered at Isaac suspiciously. "Can't you read the sign, son?"

Isaac looked again at the words on the sign and signed. "Very funny, Aunt Meg. But I'm no dick. I'm your nephew. And I'm here for honorable reasons."

"Honorable, eh?" said Aunt Meg, chuckling. "I'll be the judge of that."

She opened up the front door and Isaac tried to swallow away his judgment. She was wearing baggy gray sweatpants with holes at the knees and a stained t-shirt that said "Meh" on it.

Behind her, the hallway was full of piles of unopened mail. The wallpaper was dark and peeling — still the same paper his parents had put up thirty years ago. Now, there were damp patches and bubbles of mold on it. And as much as the whole place stank of damp and microwave French fries, there was still something about the smell that told him he was home.

"Well, don't just stand there gawping," said Aunt Meg, leading him through to the kitchen at the back of the house. "Sit down and say whatever it is you want to say."

Isaac couldn't help looking down at the spot where he'd been born, positioned directly beside the dining table. He pictured his mother gripping the edge of that table, and his father crouching beneath her, catching his slippery newborn body like he was birthing a calf.

That spot of the floor, now, was splashed with coffee stains and full of crumbs of... goodness knows what.

Isaac decided to sit on the other side of the table. Felt too strange to sit right there.

"Squirt?" said Aunt Meg, opening the fridge.

Isaac frowned. "What?"

"Soda?" said his aunt, holding up a yellow can.

"Oh, right," said Isaac. "Uh, thanks."

Over the past couple of decades, Isaac had sampled a martini with a one-carat diamond in it at a hotel in Tokyo, he'd drunk two-hundred-year-old Champagne rescued from a shipwreck, and he'd downed a shot of a rare single malt whisky kept in a gold and emerald Fabergé Celtic Egg. What he had never, ever had before was a can of Squirt with the aunt who had stolen his family home from him. But there was a first for everything.

"Refrigerator broke," she told him as the warm, flat, grapefruit-flavored soda touched his lips.

Isaac tried his very best to look *not*-disgusted.

Don't fuck this up, Isaac. You only get one chance at this.

"Well," said Isaac, turning his body away from the window at the back of the kitchen. Were he to look through that window, he might catch a glimpse of his parents' graves, and he couldn't allow that to happen. Too emotional. He didn't want Aunt Meg to see him cry.

"Well," said Aunt Meg, sitting over the spot that Isaac was born, glaring into his eyes like they were about to duel.

"I'm so sorry to hear about Uncle Jeffrey," said Isaac. "I hope that you're coping alright."

Clearly, Aunt Meg wasn't coping. The dirty dishes strewn about the kitchen. The stains and spillages all over the floor. The dark circles around her eyes.

Maybe striking this deal was going to be easier than he thought. Maybe she couldn't wait to get this place off her hands.

"Meh," said Aunt Meg, not seeming to realize that she was saying the exact same thing that was written on her t-shirt.

Isaac cleared his throat. "Listen, Aunt Meg," he said. "I know this is a tough time for you. And looking after this ranch all on your own... It must be... a challenge."

His aunt snorted.

"If you like," he said, his voice as gentle as possible, "I can take it off your hands."

Immediately, Aunt Meg's posture changed. She sat bolt upright and her eyes widened. "You couldn't help yourself, could you? Coming here, trying to steal the place now that I'm weak?"

Isaac raised his palms. "That's not my intention, madam. I'm here to help you. No offense, Aunt, but I can see that you're struggling." He gestured around the room, hoping that she could see the dirt like he could. "I'm not trying to steal the ranch from you. I want to buy it off you."

Aunt Meg's shoulders hunched slightly. She sipped from her can of Squirt, eying Isaac warily.

"Five million dollars," said Isaac, cutting to the chase. "That's a generous offer. Way more than it's worth."

Way more than it's worth since you ran it into the ground, anyway.

"Not a chance in hell," said Aunt Meg, the Squirt spitting out from between her teeth.

"Alright," said Isaac. He could see she was playing hardball. "I'll double it. Ten million."

That was a crazy offer, but who cared? Isaac had the money, and all that mattered to him was that he got the place.

Aunt Meg laughed. "Look at you, son. Throwing around these numbers like you're all that and a bag of chips. It's disgraceful. Can't you see this is my home? It's not for sale."

"Fine," said Isaac through gritted teeth. "Twenty million."

For a while, there was silence between them. Well, not complete silence. There was the sound of a fly buzzing over by the window, banging into the glass every now and then as it tried to escape.

Aunt Meg stared at him, then she chugged down the rest of her Squirt. After a loud burp, she said, "Son, you'd need to change every single thing about yourself before I even started to consider your offer."

Isaac frowned, confused. "What do you mean?"

Disgust crawled across Aunt Meg's face like a maggot on a pile of rotting flesh. "I know what you're like," she told Isaac. "I saw you grow up, remember?"

Isaac shrugged. "So?"

"I used to see you wandering around town with a different girl every night. I heard the stories of the things you used to do with those girls. Making them dress up funny and doing all sorts of unspeakable things to them." She swallowed as if trying to get rid of a bad taste.

"I don't see how—"

"And I know how you made all your money too, Isaac. I know that you run some kind of a—" she whispered, "—fetish business."

"It's not what you—"

"This is a good Christian ranch," Aunt Meg snapped. "Always has been, always will be. Your poor parents. They'd be turning over in their graves if they could see the man you became."

Isaac felt his blood starting to boil. He felt like he felt as a teenager, just after his parents had died. Powerless. Alone. Angry. His hands became fists, but he made it his mission not to let Aunt Meg see his fury. That would be game over.

"I am a Christian as it happens," Isaac said. "There's nothing wrong with expressing your sexuality and at the same time—"

"You'd have to be a married man for starters," said Aunt Meg, suddenly, standing up and staring at him with a glint in her eye.

Isaac paused, taken aback. She'd thrown him a line. But at the same time, it was an impossible one to grab hold of. "You know I'm not the marrying type."

Aunt Meg smiled wickedly. "Oh dear. Guess you'll never get the ranch then."

Isaac took a long, deep breath. He was shaking. He was fuming. He wasn't used to being told 'no'.

"What's the matter, Isaac?" his aunt taunted him. "The thought of settling down with just one girl makes your blood run cold? Got too many wild oats to sow?"

Isaac stood up, looking down at his aunt. "I offered you an opportunity," he told her. "An opportunity to buy whatever you wanted for the rest of your life. All the Squirt your heart desired. Shares in the damn *company*, if you wanted. Clothes with slogans on them. Vacations. Cars. Happiness." He composed himself. "But you threw away that opportunity, Aunt Meg. And you're throwing away this ranch with it. Those cattle out there are close to death. And this land won't be fit for anything if you let it fall apart much more."

Aunt Meg blinked at him, unmoved. "Guess that's just the way it's gotta be."

Isaac could taste the bitterness in his throat. He wanted this ranch almost as much as he wanted oxygen. It was his. It didn't make sense that his aunt got to keep it. His parents always told him it would be his when they died.

"Think about it," said Isaac. "Twenty million dollars. My offer stays open."

"So does mine." Aunt Meg crossed her arms. "Get married or go home."

Go home.

This *was* his home.

Isaac said goodbye with a heavy feeling inside, like he'd just eaten a lump of lead.

As he walked out of the ranch, he thought about how different things would have been if this place was his. Green grass. Fresh air. Fat, happy cattle with a load of happy fat, happy ranchers looking after them. He wouldn't deal with the animals himself, of course, because of his allergy, but that was okay. He could play to his strengths. Build some kind of lucrative side hustle on the land: a dude ranch or a luxury hotel, with a small cabin tucked away at the back of the grounds. Somewhere for him to relax at the weekends. Maybe, if he'd had this place, he'd never have gone to Miami at all.

He didn't even look at Aunt Meg as he stepped out of the front door. But he couldn't resist walking around the side of the building after he left her, to take a look at his parents' graves. Maybe say a few quick words to them before Aunt Meg kicked him off the property.

As soon as he turned the corner, though, he froze. His parents' graves were there. He could still see the wooden crosses over the spot they'd been put in the ground. But Aunt Meg had dumped something on top of the graves: an old, dirty mattress.

Immediately, a hot fire of determination began to burn in the pit of his stomach.

This wasn't the end.

It was just the beginning.

He'd do whatever it took. He'd do it for them.

Chapter Four

PEACH

PEACH AND KIERA WALKED barefoot along the beach. They'd both left their shoes back at the hotel, because you could do things like that in Miami. Peach was wearing a PAW Patrol t-shirt and PAW Patrol shorts, and Kiera wore a neon pink sundress. Peach rarely wore dresses because she was self-conscious about her figure. She was definitely on the curvier side, though her friends always assured her that her body was catnip for men.

Peach was carrying a bag of buckets and spades and they were looking for exactly the right spot to make the world's biggest sandcastle.

"This beach is the best," said Kiera.

Peach agreed. "Teddy seems to like it too."

Teddy *adored* the beach. He was running around in circles, barking in that ear-piercing way of his that Peach had learned to love.

"Well, who wouldn't?" said Kiera. "It's paradise here. I love everything about it."

"Except that jerk from Daisy's office. What was his name again? Isaac." Peach pretended like it took her a minute to remember Isaac's name, but it didn't. He'd been on her mind almost constantly since yesterday. She was still feeling sore about the way he'd spoken to her.

Getting told off was always upsetting, but getting told off by a handsome billionaire was upsetting *and* confusing. She didn't know why, but she'd woken up having a dirty dream about Isaac. She'd felt it so strongly — his face buried deep between her thighs, eating her up like she was a warm slice of pie. She hadn't told Daisy or Kiera about it, though. Much too weird.

"Oh yeah. Except for that meanie," Kiera agreed.

Peach was eager to change the subject. "I kinda wish I didn't have to go back to Connecticut."

Kiera stopped walking all of a sudden, grabbing on to Peach's arm. "I feel the same way! I feel like I could just stay here forever."

Peach giggled. "Maybe we're Miami girls deep down. We were born in the wrong town. Now, we need to make it our lifelong mission to return to the place we belong." She was playing, but Kiera wasn't laughing.

"Life without Daisy has been weird," said Kiera, kicking the sand. "Home just doesn't feel like home anymore."

Peach tried not to take offense at this. It's not like she didn't get what Kiera was saying, but she still felt a pang of jealousy when Kiera said it. Kiera had always seemed to prefer Daisy to her, and it was hard not to feel like Kiera thought Connecticut was boring with just Peach for company. Maybe it was just the fact that Peach had low self-esteem. She often read the worst into a situation.

"I'm sure when we get home we'll be glad to be back," said Peach, trying to sound cheerful. "Lobster rolls. Steamed cheeseburgers. Apple cider." She handed Kiera a bucket and spade and they sat down on the sand, making sandcastles together.

Neither of them said anything for a while, but it felt obvious to Peach that they were both thinking hard about what they'd just been talking about.

"You know, I don't think I really *need* to go back home," said Kiera, finally breaking the silence.

Peach squashed the sandcastle she was making. All her sandcastles were coming out wonky, while Kiera's were perfect. She looked at her friend. "What do you mean? Your whole life is back there. Your apartment. Your work. You can't stay on vacation forever."

Kiera carefully added a sandcastle on top of another sandcastle. "Thing is," she said, "I could run my bubble bath company from anywhere. All I need is a room to make my bubble bath. And a computer to advertise it. So why not do it here? As much key lime pie as I want... for the rest of my life!" She let out an evil cackle.

Peach tried to join in with the fun, but it was hard. She *didn't* have a job that could be done from Miami. Sure, she could apply to sweep up dog hair clippings at a different groomer's out here, but... what about the animal shelter? She'd volunteered at that place for years. The doggies relied on her. There was Woody the three-legged German Shepherd, Billy the blind bulldog, Bandit the Jack Russell with PTSD. They weren't easy dogs to look after, but Peach had a way with them. They trusted her. She couldn't just move to Miami and leave them all behind.

She looked over at Teddy, happily running around them in circles. If it hadn't been for the shelter, Teddy would never have come into her life. She couldn't turn her back on Connecticut. Definitely not just on a whim.

"You look like you're about to tell me you could never leave home," Kiera said.

"The rescue home—" Peach began.

"They don't even pay you. And as for the grooming place, it's slave labor! You could find a better job here. Hey, maybe you could even work for Daddies Inc?"

"For Isaac?" blurted Peach. "No way."

"Well, you could do anything!" said Kiera, spreading her arms wide.

Peach shook her head. "You can't just reinvent your life in the blink of an eye. I'm just not destined for this life, Kiera. Daisy got lucky. She ran away from Mr. Wrong and bumped straight into Mr. Right. But... I'm destined to clean up dog clippings forevermore. And if I let myself dream any bigger than that, it'll just lead to disappointment."

"I thought you seemed inspired by our tour of the Daddies Inc offices yesterday. You had this look in your eye, like anything was possible."

"And then I got told off for bringing my pet into the building and I realized that people with big dreams are generally a-holes." She dug a hole in the sand and buried her feet in it. Teddy ran over to her and began barking, as if alerting her to the fact that she was trapped. "It's okay, Teddy," she said. "See?" She pulled out her feet and wiggled her sandy toes. Teddy licked them, sand and all. "Ew!"

"I dunno," said Kiera. "I... think I might do it. I'm my own boss, after all. I'm going to let myself dream big. I'll extend my stay for a few days and look for someplace to live. I love you, Peach, but my life has felt so empty lately."

Peach felt the color drain from her cheeks.

"Not because of you, Peach!" Kiera said quickly. "I love you! You know that. I just... haven't felt all that fulfilled lately. I feel like I'm stagnating. I feel like I need to try something new... You sure you don't want in on this?"

Quietly, she said, "Kiera. Seriously. My entire life is in Connecticut. One of my best friends already left. And now you say you're leaving too."

"But you should come with me!" Kiera lifted her bucket to reveal yet another perfect sandcastle.

"I can't," Peach sniffed. "I can't afford to quit my job. I can't just be spontaneous like you. Plus, the rescue center brings me happiness. I have to live in reality. Not some fantasy world where I get to do whatever I want and start over. I had to do that after my parents kicked me out for being a Little. Starting from scratch. I'm not doing it again."

Kiera looked defeated. "Fine," she said. "I get it. You think I'm crazy. But you'll see. I'm joining Daisy for the good life." Kiera paused. "And obviously you can come stay with me any time you like. In fact, I insist that you do. But I *am* moving here."

With those words, Peach felt yet another friend drifting away from her. Well, not so much drifting away as running away as fast as her legs would carry her, and slamming the door in Peach's face.

Chapter Five

ISAAC

T HERE WERE SEVERAL REASONS that Isaac didn't want to go back to his Miami compound. Number one: having been back to the ranch, nowhere else felt like home. Number two: seeing his aunt so lonely, rattling around in that big old ranch house... it made him feel strange about rattling around on *his* own now too. Number three: the damn cat was still there.

He'd gotten a message from his PA, Charlotte, this morning. Animal control weren't interested in coming to collect a stray kitten. They had too much on their hands, and they told Isaac to try to find a home for the cat himself. Isaac had asked Charlotte to take it, but she told him her greyhounds would rip it to shreds in a hot second. She'd brought over a litter tray and some food and a bed and told Isaac he was going to have to look after it until he found it somewhere to live.

For that reason, then, Isaac was avoiding going home. For one thing, he had allergies, and now that the kitten was roaming his house, all its skin cells and saliva and fur would be shedding around the place, and Isaac would get sick immediately. It felt like his home had been invaded. Which was exactly how he felt about his aunt living on his family ranch.

Damn.

He needed a drink.

He swung into the Dade-D Bar — a Daddies-Inc-owned age-play drinkery in Miami-Dade — looking for a familiar face. Cindy was working behind the bar but Montague and Bastion weren't here. Montague rarely came out now he had Daisy to look after. It's not like Isaac was annoyed about that. He got it. Daddies had a responsibility toward their Littles. And Daisy had been through so much with her ex. It was good that Montague was caring for her so well. It's just... well, the three of them used to be like the three amigos. Single and ready to mingle. Talking business, shooting the shit, necking drinks, and going to clubs together. Without Montague, Bastion and Isaac never seemed to make the effort to meet up socially. Montague was like the glue that had kept them all together.

"How's it going, boss?" asked Cindy. "Long day?"

Isaac smiled. "Is it that obvious?"

Cindy knew what Isaac liked to drink, and poured him a martini on the rocks, decorated with an olive. The Littles never drank alcohol here. They came for the freakshakes. Cindy made the most decadent drinks around. But after the day Isaac had had, he needed something strong.

"So, what's up?" Cindy asked him.

"Oh, you know," said Isaac. He was never one to discuss his problems with other people. "Just... business."

He had to try and think of it like that. That's all this stuff with his aunt was: business. He'd gone to her with an offer. She'd made a counter-offer. Her counter-offer was ridiculous. He'd left.

That's just how it goes in the world of business.

You win some, you lose some.

Isaac wasn't fooling anyone though, least of all himself. He felt like shit.

"You look almost as miserable as her," said Cindy, pointing at a Little in the corner of the room. Isaac caught sight of the back of her. She wore her strawberry blond hair in bunches. Her clothes were all pastel-colored and plastered with cartoon characters. Isaac was a Daddy Dom, but he had never been into cutsey Littles like that. He preferred quiet Middles, or occasionally Littles who were so far regressed they just drank their milk and crawled about and never said a word. Littles like the one over there, sucking her thumb and sulking about something — they were trouble.

Just then, the Little he was staring at turned around.

"Wait," he said, "I recognize her."

"That's Daisy's friend Peach," said Cindy. "She's been in here for hours. She's had three freakshakes and I'm worried she's gonna barf all over my nice velvet chairs."

Isaac looked at the girl, who had that daft dog of hers perched on her lap, and he felt his hands ball into fists. "Leave it to me."

He marched toward the girl, ready to tell her that it was time to leave. Not only had she had enough to drink, but she'd also brought her dog into another Daddies Inc establishment. It's not that dogs weren't allowed in the bar... but there was no sign that said that they *were*.

"Hey," said Isaac. "Peach isn't it?"

Peach looked up at him, and it was clear that she'd been crying. Heaps.

Immediately, Isaac felt a rush of protective energy. Okay, so sexually, his preference was for Littles who were a lot less high-maintenance than this one, but he was still a Daddy deep down. And Littles needed looking after.

His tone softened. "I'm Isaac. We met the other day. Daisy's friend, right?"

Peach shrugged.

"Mind if I sit here a moment?" Isaac asked, pulling out a chair.

Peach's posture stiffened. She put her arms around her dog protectively. "Are you going to throw me out again, sir? The woman behind the bar said it was fine to bring my dog in here. Teddy's harmless. And he's very clean, even though he doesn't necessarily look it—"

"What's up, Little girl?" Isaac cut in as gently as possible. "Cindy tells me you've been downing milkshake like there's no tomorrow, and you look... well, frankly, you look a little lost."

Peach screwed up her nose. "Why do you care? You were very rude to me the other day. You clearly hate me and my dog."

Isaac could already feel his nose tingling and his eyes itching. Goddammit. There was no escape from little furry critters these days. He moved his chair back a little, getting some more distance between him and the allergens.

"I don't hate your dog," said Isaac. Which was mostly true. He didn't *hate* cats and dogs. He just hated the effect they had on him. And maybe, over the years, he'd come to demonize them because of that. Who the hell knew? He wasn't a psychologist. "But I don't believe dogs should be allowed in public places unless they're dogs for the blind."

"Why?" asked Peach, blinking at him. "Animals are our friends. Also, I don't know if you heard me before, but Teddy's hypoallergenic. Teddy wouldn't do anyone a bit of harm."

As if trying to prove its innocence, the dog barked, and it was the ugliest, most ear-piercing noise that Isaac had ever heard.

Trying to ignore the feeling in his ears, like they'd just been pricked with pins, Isaac said: "I can assure you I've heard it all before. It's hypoallergenic. It doesn't shed much. It's perfectly safe... Nope. Not where I'm concerned. I'm allergic to all creatures, period."

"Including humans?" Peach asked quietly.

Isaac decided it was best to just change the subject. "Where are your friends, young lady? Daisy has been so excited about having her friends come to stay with her. I thought you'd all be off exploring the city together."

Peach snorted. "I'm not really one of Daisy's friends anymore."

Uh oh. Isaac was worried about this. Littles needed friends. Peach was all alone in a big new city, and that meant that she could end up in all kinds of trouble. Three milkshakes in a row was just the start of the inevitable downward spiral.

"Want to talk about it?" said Isaac. "I have time."

Even if it means having to sit here with your dog to avoid my cat.

Not that it's my cat.

There's just no way I'm keeping that damn furball.

"I don't know," said Peach, shaking her head. "I don't know you that well. And I don't get why you care."

Isaac nodded. "That's fair. We didn't get off to the best start. And I'm not much of a people person. Not like Montague or Bastion. But I care because you're a Little. And I care about Littles. Even Littles with—" Isaac looked down at Teddy, "—hellhounds."

Peach's jaw dropped. "Teddy's not a hellhound! But... I guess I could talk to you. I don't have much choice now that my friends have gone."

"Where did they go?" asked Isaac.

"They're at a beauty spa," Peach replied. "No dogs allowed."

Isaac bit his lip, resisting the urge to make a comment.

"Thing is, they keep doing things together without me. They say I'm invited, but I can't go anywhere without Teddy." She sniffed. "And now Kiera is talking about moving here, to be with Daisy. Daisy used to be *my* best friend, and, and, and—" Peach's lower lip began trembling, and soon she was crying her eyes out, with snot pouring out of her nose and down onto her cartoon t-shirt.

The strange thing was, Isaac wasn't turned off by it in the least. In fact, he found Peach's childlike vulnerability strangely charming. He passed her a napkin.

"Sounds like this vacation hasn't been going like you planned," said Isaac. "Friends can be difficult, eh? Especially when there are three of you. One of you often gets left out." Isaac thought about Montague and Bastion. How Montague had been too busy with Daisy lately to hang out. How Bastion was too busy getting his dick wet with a bunch of strangers to meet up. Isaac was the one that always got left out too. The lonely one. The one whose dick remained dry as a bone.

"It's not just that, though," said Peach. "My whole life is in disarray. Back home in Connecticut, I somehow managed to switch off my brain. Tell myself that I was happy with my lot. But you know what? I've got nothing. And there's so much I want."

Isaac leaned forward. "Like what?"

Peach looked at him. "I'd like to be successful. To be financially independent enough to spend my whole time volunteering if I wanted to. And I'd like to travel."

Isaac smiled. "Where would you go first?"

"Europe," Peach replied, quick as a whip. "Probably Spain. I think it seems so romantic. The twiddly guitar music. The pink drinks. The big juicy oranges."

Isaac nodded, looking at the cocktail umbrella in Peach's empty glass. He couldn't believe this, but there was an idea forming. "Hey," he said slowly, carefully, "how about we strike a... business deal?"

Peach blew her nose and then frowned at him, confused. "What are you talking about, sir?"

"A simple financial transaction," said Isaac, the idea becoming clearer with each passing second. It was so obvious now that he couldn't believe he hadn't had it before. "I'd like to pay you a lot of money," he said, "in return for marrying me."

Peach's eyes widened. "You're... proposing to me?"

"Purely a business agreement," Isaac said quickly. Without meaning for it to happen, his gaze slipped down to Peach's ample bosom, her curvaceous figure. He found himself imagining her generous body under all that bright clothing. What someone as colorful as her would be like in the sack. Then, he forced himself to stop. "This wouldn't be a sexual thing."

It *couldn't* be a sexual thing. Sex was complicated. This plan was simple. Sex would ruin the whole thing. Besides, plump, excitable little Peach wasn't his type. And he definitely wasn't hers, either.

Peach looked thoughtfully at him, slipping her finger into her mouth thoughtfully.

Damn, girl. Don't do that. It makes me think about...

"It wouldn't be a sexual thing," said Isaac, his cock thickening in his pants. He had images of sliding his dick between her large, bouncy breasts, then pushing it up to her lips, his balls resting on her bosom as she sucked him hard. "It's simply a legal agreement. The marriage will be in place for long enough for me to buy my family ranch."

Peach took her finger out of her mouth. It glistened with her saliva. "You need to be married to buy your family ranch?"

"It's a long story," Isaac replied. "But as soon as I buy the ranch, we can get the marriage annulled. It's quick and easy if you never actually... consummate the marriage."

Peach began twirling her hair with her wet finger. She leaned forward, elbows on the table as she did so, listening intently. The t-shirt wasn't a low-cut one, but it was clearly a kids' size, and given Peach's ample figure, it was tight on her, showing every bulge. Isaac couldn't believe he was having all these thoughts about her. He'd never looked twice at a curvy girl before. And now... now, he was having visions of smearing her body with the remains of that chocolate milkshake, then licking it off her, bit by bit...

"We'll have to make it seem real while it lasts," said Isaac. "We'll be the only two people who know the truth. So, no telling our friends it's fake. And you'll move into my compound to make it seem real. But you can have your own mansion."

"My own mansion?" Peach asked.

"Yeah. I have four," Isaac said with a shrug. "So, what do you say? Easiest money you'll ever make."

Peach narrowed her eyes. "How much?"

"Two million," he said, without skipping a beat. Being a numbers guy, Isaac knew that as nice as a million dollars was, it wouldn't necessarily set Peach up for life. Not if she wanted financial independence and luxury.

Peach looked at him blankly. "Two million dollars. To pretend to be married to you."

Isaac was used to playing hardball. "Alright. Five million."

Peach shook her head wildly.

"Fine," he said, taking a deep breath. "Ten million."

He really had to stop upping his figures like this. Normally he was much more restrained. This was just so emotional for him. His family ranch. He had to beat his aunt at all costs. And Peach seemed like the perfect accomplice. She needed the money. He knew her friends, so she couldn't just disappear off the face of the planet. And, like it or not, his cock wanted him to choose her.

Peach waved her hands in the air. "Stop. Stop! I'll do it!"

Isaac was taken aback. "You will?"

"I will," said Peach. "I'll marry you."

Was it Isaac's imagination, or did *her* gaze travel down *his* body now? He hoped she didn't notice the bulge at his groin. He really didn't know why the idea of fake-marrying this strange Little girl was making his cock so engorged. No business transaction, even the most exciting ones, had ever given him a boner before.

Suddenly, he was brought back to reality by the sight of the dirty little dog reaching its paws up to Peach's shoulders and giving her mouth a lick.

Ew.

"There's just one condition," Isaac said, looking at Teddy. "The mutt is allowed on my compound, but it never enters my home."

Peach looked down at Teddy and then back at Isaac. Then she looked at Teddy again.

"I... I can't do this," she said. "Not with someone like you. I'm sorry."

With that, she grabbed her PAW Patrol backpack and ran out of the bar with her dog yelping in her arms.

Isaac watched her butt wobble as she ran out.

He knew it had been too good to be true. A girl like her — young and cute and bubbly — would never be interested in marrying a man like him. Not even for ten million dollars.

Chapter Six

PEACH

"ARE YOU SURE YOU want to leave?" Kiera asked Peach, hugging her tight.

Daisy joined in the hug. "You know we'd love for you to come and live here too!"

Peach noticed that word. "We." Daisy and Kiera were already a "we."

Gone were the days of private messages relayed in Gigglish. Gone were the days of meeting at the ice-cream parlor after work. Gone were the days of living within a thousand miles of her best friends. Gone were the days, most likely, of having best friends.

It's not that Peach didn't appreciate Daisy and Kiera bringing her to the airport like this. It was just... a bit much. They had both chosen to leave her, after all. It was hard not to think that they'd come to see her off at the airport just to be sure that she was really gone.

"I really wish you'd reconsider," said Kiera, pulling away, her cheeks stained with tears. "We'll miss you so much."

For about five minutes you will. Then you'll head off to the spa and forget all about me.

"It's true," said Daisy. "We're a three. Not a two. And I just know you'd love Miami."

Peach shook her head. "They need me at the rescue center."

"They treat you like dog poop there," Kiera chimed in. "Free labor for years. You're the only member of staff who doesn't get paid."

"The *dogs* need me," said Peach. She looked down at Teddy in the little carrier she had to keep him in for the flight. He looked grumpy about it already. She wondered how he'd cope after another hour. Two hours. Three.

"You've already helped all those animals a bunch," Daisy said. "There are animals that need saving in Miami too, you know."

For some reason, Peach thought about Isaac. Was he an animal that needed saving? When he'd spoken to her yesterday, there was a strange air about him. Peach wondered if he was one of those people that lacked empathy. Maybe not a sociopath and definitely not a psychopath, but there was definitely a barrier between him and the world. And the way he threw those figures around like they meant nothing...

Besides, what kind of person would offer to marry someone for ten million dollars? It was crazy. And why did he hate Teddy so much? Teddy was the best. It was basically *impossible* to hate Teddy. Maybe he *was* a psychopath, after all.

On the other hand, what kind of crazy person would *turn down* the offer of ten million dollars to marry someone? She'd have had an entire mansion to herself to live in. She'd have had so much money she could have *bought* the rescue center twice over. She could have started her own charity, and dreamed bigger than she ever thought possible. The old Peach would have been back in business. Ambitious Peach.

And she wouldn't have had to have sex with him either. This wasn't some shady *Pretty Woman* type arrangement. She just had to sign a piece of paper and that was that.

And yet...

The way he'd looked at Teddy filled her with sadness. Because for a moment, she'd gotten herself excited. She'd read enough romance novels to know that when a handsome, grumpy guy asks you to enter into a marriage contract with you, it can only mean one thing... sex-o-rama!

But not with someone like Isaac.

Even if he did have the most muscly-looking body she'd ever seen. And these intense brown eyes that seemed to be undressing her as they spoke.

Still. Isaac was a bad man. And she... well, she was an animal-loving Little who ate way too many cookies and drank way too many milkshakes and was destined for a life alone on the couch watching cartoons. She wasn't like Daisy. Daisy was the kind of pretty Little who Daddy Doms raved over. Blond hair, sunshiney personality. Peach was just a poor girl from the suburbs who barely fit in her jeans and who spoke like one of the members of PAW Patrol.

"I've made up my mind," said Peach. "I need to go back home."

Kiera took a deep breath. "I'll probably be back in a few days, too. This is probably just a ridiculous pipe dream. You know me, with my big ideas..."

I have big ideas too, Peach wanted to scream. But she didn't. She just swallowed them away like she swallowed an entire pack of cookies this morning.

"I'll come out to stay in the houseboat in a month or two," Daisy told her. "When Daddy can get time off work to come visit." Daisy reached into her pocket and pulled out a hundred-dollar bill. "This is from Daddy, actually. He said to get yourself something nice from the departure lounge."

"I can't take this," said Peach sadly.

Daisy nodded. "Yes you can. You can pay the money back when I next see you." She smiled kindly.

Ugh. Everyone knew Peach was broke. They were all trying to throw money at her. It was embarrassing. Kiera had even paid for her flight here.

"Alright," Peach said, taking the note. "But I'm definitely paying you back."

Peach hugged her friends again and watched them walk away, and she couldn't help but feel like she'd just been paid off.

*

What do you do with a hundred dollars when you have an hour to kill at the airport? The choice was too great. Peach worked out that she could buy fifty-nine Krispy Kreme donuts. Or she could buy herself seventy-two choc chip cookies. Or ninety-nine cans of cola.

But she wanted something longer-lasting. Something to remind her of her stay here. A souvenir from the worst trip of a lifetime. So, she found herself gravitating toward Build-A-Bear. The cool thing about Build-A-Bear was that they didn't just sell bears. They had a PAW Patrol stuffie of Chase, and Peach had always wanted the money to buy one.

She went into the store with a guilty feeling in the pit of her stomach. It felt so extravagant to buy something like this. She bought PAW Patrol clothes and had a branded backpack too, but she always bought them second-hand. Most of them were dirty or ripped and none of them fit her quite right.

This stuffie was going to be brand-new.

As the assistant walked her through all the different options, her mind whirled. What clothes did she want? A rainbow stripe dress, of course. What accessories? A guacamole wristie, naturally. And what about the sound? And the scent? The PAW Patrol theme tune. And bubblegum.

She took the finished stuffie up to the counter, faintly amused with herself. What had started out as a guilty pleasure had turned into a really fun experience. Chase looked silly as heck but that was part of the fun. What shocked her was how much he cost. Almost all her money had gone on one stuffed toy! She could have kept that money for rent or for heating or for treats for the dogs at the rescue center, but you know what? It felt good to treat herself for once.

She walked out of the store, swinging the bag happily in one hand, and holding Teddy nice and steady in the other.

"What shall I get with my last thirteen dollars, Teddy? Something sensible like a salad?"

She looked down and saw that Teddy was asleep. He did that sometimes when he got stressed. So did she, to be fair.

"Nah," she said to herself. "I'll get seven donuts. And with the remaining sixty cents I'll buy a lettuce." She laughed a hollow laugh.

It wasn't really fair when she thought about it. How come someone as good at math as she was had ended up with no money? And how come someone as fun as she was had ended up with no friends?

I should take this ridiculous stuffie back to the store and get a refund, she thought sadly. *Save the money for something important.*

But as much as she wanted to head back to the shop and feel that hundred dollars safely back in her pocket, she found that she couldn't move. She was completely frozen to the spot. Her fingers were firmly clasped around the handle of the bag.

This could just be the beginning, Peach, she said to herself. *A drop in the ocean.*

She visualized ten million dollars, which was actually way too much money to visualize. In her head, it kinda looked like that huge heap of gold coins Scrooge McDuck swam around in the cartoon *Duck Tales*.

Why shouldn't she get a turn at being Scrooge?

What was so wrong with that?

Quick as a flash, she put down the dog carrier, and she sent a text message to Daisy.

What's Isaac's number?

Before she even got her answer, she said under her breath, "PAW Patrol is on a roll!"

*

The cab ride to Isaac's place was... interesting. Peach only had thirteen dollars in her pocket, and she knew that wouldn't cover the ride. She just had to hope and pray that Isaac would pay the fare.

She was also taking a great big leap of faith in doing this. She messaged the dog grooming parlor to tell them to stick their job where the sun don't shine. Actually, she didn't say it like that because she was a good girl. She wrote a long, sweet email about how it was time for her to find her true calling. (Her true calling happened to be ten million dollars, but she didn't mention that part.)

Then, she messaged the rescue center, which was a whole lot harder. She told them she wouldn't be volunteering for a while, but would be back when she could. It just didn't feel right ending things completely with them. Maybe when she was a multimillionaire she'd head back there and do the odd shift. Working as a volunteer would be so much more fun if she had a millionaire's mansion to go back to at the end of the day. She just had to be careful not to take every single dog back home with her...

YES DADDY   45

Daisy kept sending Peach text messages during the cab ride, but Peach decided not to answer them.

Why did you ask for Isaac's number?

Are you going to send him an angry text?

Are you still sore about the thing with Teddy?

I promise you, Isaac's a good guy.

Wait. Is HE the reason you left?

Eventually, Daisy stopped messaging. Peach hadn't said a word to her friends about Isaac's (literal) proposal, of course. They just didn't feel like part of her inner circle anymore. Too wrapped up in each other. Plus, it felt kinda good to keep a secret from them. They seemed to have so many secrets from her now. Going off on their private trips without her. Pretty soon, they'd have shut her out entirely. So, in a way, this was... payback?

"What did you say you're doing on Star Island again?" the cab driver said, casting her yet another glance in his rearview mirror. He seemed totally confused about how someone who looked like Peach could be headed to the most exclusive spot in all of Miami.

Peach wasn't offended by his confusion. She knew how she looked. Wearing her cartoonish kids' clothes, which happened to have Nutella smeared all over them from this morning's breakfast. Her blond hair tied in a messy bun. No make-up. A scruffy little dog for her travel companion.

Peach was out of place. Major time. But with ten million dollars coming her way... did it really matter?

"I'm meeting my future husband," she told the cab driver, trying to hide a smile.

"Sure you are," replied the driver. "Just remember the island has tight security there. Name's gotta be on the list to get in. Can't have any Tom, Dick, or Sally waltzing in and knocking on Angelina Jolie's door."

Peach gasped. "Angeline Jolie lives on the island?"

The driver shrugged. "Nobody knows who lives on the island. That's the whole point. It's extremely exclusive. And private." He cast her another look, an expression of warning this time.

"Don't you worry about that," said Peach. "My fiancée will be ecstatic to see me."

The driver grunted.

Peach's tummy was doing backflips. A celebrity island! She couldn't help getting out her phone and googling who lived there. According to the internet... Gloria Estefan, Jennifer Lopez, some pharmaceutical billionaire named Philip Frost... No mention of Isaac, but presumably the Daddies Inc guys were careful about putting their names out to the general public. Not everyone appreciated the age play community, so you had to stay guarded.

And what better place to do that than on an exclusive Miami island?

As the cab began driving across the bridge that led to the island, Peach tried to control her excitement. For one thing, her bladder was pretty full and she didn't want to pee in her panties. For another, she had to remind herself why she was doing this. It wasn't because she wanted to hang out with A-list celebrities or buy herself endless fancy necklaces and Build-A-Bear toys.

No. She was doing this because she wanted to have *impact*. She had always been Peach, the childish overweight girl who nobody took seriously. The overly generous girl who people took advantage of because she was too scared to stand up for herself.

Not anymore. Peach was about to get rich with a capital "R" and she was going to use that money *very* wisely. And if she bought herself the occasional stuffie or necklace for a bit of self-care, that hardly made her a bad person, did it?

They pulled up to some security gates, and the cab driver rolled down Peach's window.

"Name?" asked the guard. He was wearing dark glasses and looked like someone you didn't mess with.

"Um, Peach Trimble, sir," said Peach quietly.

The guard looked at her a moment.

"Ms. Trimble," he said sternly.

Peach could feel the cab driver's eyes boring into her.

"Welcome to Star Island," said the guard.

Peach felt like she could breathe again, and the security gates opened.

The driver tried to hide his bemusement as he drove them across the length of the island. They passed mansion after mansion, each one more stunning than the next. Extravagant gates leading to the most stunning courtyards and pillared entrances.

Finally, they reached Isaac's compound, and as soon as the cab approached, the gates opened. Very cool.

The cab took them all the way up to the door and Peach nodded graciously at the driver.

He looked at her, as if weighing something up, then said: "Two hundred dollars."

"Two hundred? For a cab ride?" Peach said, aghast.

The driver chuckled. "What's the matter? You can clearly afford it."

"I just need to... um... go ask..."

"You're full of shit," the cab driver spat, his whole demeanor changing. "This is some kind of setup, isn't it? You cheated your way to getting your name on that list. You don't belong here."

Just then, the hand-carved front door of the imposing mansion ahead of her opened. And out stepped Isaac.

He was wearing a linen shirt with the sleeves rolled up and blue jeans. He looked totally different to the last times she'd seen him, in business attire. This was relaxing-at-home Isaac, and if it wasn't for the fact he was a full-on animal-hater, he'd have looked very sexy. That clean-shaven face showing off his strong jawline. The floppy brown hair. The wide chest. He looked like a Daddy from a magazine.

Isaac walked up to the cab and knocked on the driver's window.

"Is there a problem, sir?" asked Isaac.

"She's lied her way onto your property, sir," said the cab driver. "And now she won't pay me."

Isaac scowled at the driver. "*She* happens to be my fiancée," he said. "And she doesn't need to pay you a cent. I'm the one who looks after her."

Isaac reached deep into his pocket and pulled out a hundred-dollar bill. "That's more than enough to cover your costs," he told the driver.

The driver's mouth flapped open and then shut again. He took the money with a sigh. "You rich people are all the same. Tighter than a nun's asshole."

Isaac didn't seem to have heard. He was too busy opening the back door of the cab and helping Peach out. He took hold of her Build-A-Bear bag, an he took hold of Teddy, and he even gave Peach a kiss on the cheek.

"I'm so glad you're here," he said. "Let me show you your new home, future Mrs. Righton."

Peach shook her head. She could have pinched herself. Was this really the same Isaac? Maybe married life wasn't going to be so bad after all...

*

"This is my place," said Isaac, showing Peach inside. "Obviously, you won't be staying here. And nor will your dog."

Peach looked back at Teddy sadly. Isaac had insisted that Teddy stay out on the front doorstep. Teddy looked back at her with his one big eye. Poor thing. She'd get him soon.

She looked back at the entrance hall of Isaac's home. It was ridiculously grand. A huge staircase. Limestone. Marble. Chandeliers.

"Wow," she breathed. "It's like... Daddy Warbucks' mansion."

Except he's not Daddy Warbucks. He's Daddy Righton. And he's not my Daddy. He never will be.

"How many bedrooms have you got?" Peach asked, then immediately kicked herself for talking about bedrooms. She didn't want to sound like she was thinking about... that.

"Five," Isaac replied.

"But you have way more than five doors up there!" Peach said, pointing to the long row of doors at the top of the stairs.

"Well, each room has its own bathroom," said Isaac. "And there's a gym. A movie theater. Plus a bunch of other stuff."

"Other stuff?"

Isaac's eyelid twitched slightly. A tiny movement, but Peach noticed it right away. "Well, downstairs," he said, "I have a normal kitchen, a chef's kitchen, a pool, a swim-up bar, a—"

"I can hardly take this all in," said Peach. "You really live like this?"

Isaac shrugged. "You will too, babygirl. For as long as we're married."

Peach felt her entire body turn to Jell-O. No man had ever called her "babygirl" before. It felt good. Even if it was coming from *him*.

"I'll give you the grand tour sometime," said Isaac. "But right now, it's time to show you your place."

"Oh sure!" said Peach, glad of the distraction. "My place. Shall I bring Teddy?"

"Alright," said Isaac. "But we'll go around the side way. That way the creature doesn't have to enter my house."

The creature. My house. Isaac had this way of making Peach feel on top of the world and squashed under the weight of it all at once.

"Follow me," said Isaac. "I hope I chose the right mansion for you."

Oh yeah. The guy has *four* mansions on his compound. How the other half live! She guessed he'd chosen her the smallest one. Maybe the one with the worst view. But when she headed across the beautiful courtyard separating her place from his, she gasped.

Chapter Seven

ISAAC

"YOU SAID YOU ALWAYS wanted to go to Europe," said Isaac. "I figured the Mediterranean-inspired mansion was for you."

Peach's jaw was practically on the floor. It was good to see her looking excited about this. They hadn't exactly gotten off to the best start, and it was important to Isaac that this business deal of theirs was good for both of them. He didn't want Peach to feel exploited. This agreement had to be as much for her as it was for him. She was doing him a huge favor, after all.

"It's... it's... astounding," said Peach, looking up at the terracotta-colored stucco walls, the red roof tiles, the arched doorways and windows.

"Glad you like it," Isaac replied. "It's been sitting here empty since I bought the compound. It'll be good to have someone living in it for a while."

Honestly, Isaac had never really known what to make of this mansion. The other mansions on the compound were all contemporary and American in style. This one stood out a bit. He'd thought about converting it to look like all the others, but it did have a certain charm. The gas-powered lanterns outside the front door. The wrought-iron railings on the balconies. Shutters on the windows. It was cute. He could probably make some good money renting it out to vacationing A-Listers at some point. Yet another money-making idea to add to the list.

"It'll be like being on permanent vacation!" said Peach, putting down her dog carrier and facing it toward the house. "What do you think, Teddy? Shall we pretend we're living in Spain while we're here?"

The dog barked and Isaac tried not to be annoyed at the noise. Luckily, this house was far enough away from his that he wouldn't be able to hear it once it was inside. It felt strange to him to think about a dog living in one of his houses. He'd have to give it a deep clean when all this was over.

"Go on," said Isaac, handing Peach a key. "Take a look inside."

Peach opened the front door and gasped again. "It's... it's... paradise!"

Inside, this house was very different to Isaac's. His was very open, with high ceilings and a sweeping staircase. This place was built around a central courtyard with an olive tree growing in the center of it. There were stone walls, pillars, and heaps of natural colors.

"While you're on the compound, I'd appreciate it if you could restrict your dog to this outdoor space," said Isaac. "And make sure you clean up after him."

He looked down at the creature in the carrier. How could such a tiny animal make his eyes itch so badly?

"Okay," said Peach. "It's not that big of a space, but I guess I can take him for walks along the beach when he needs exercise."

"Yes," replied Isaac. "Any time you need to get anywhere, you can just call your personal driver. I left a bunch of numbers for you on the kitchen countertop. You also have a personal shopper, a masseuse, a financial adviser, a cleaner, a personal trainer, a doctor, a life coach, and a chef. Oh, and a dog-sitter."

"Seriously? All of that? A life coach? My own personal chef?"

"Of course," said Isaac with a shrug. "It's important I look after your nutritional requirements while you're on my property. In fact, it's important I look after your every need. You're my responsibility while you're here."

My responsibility. Not my Little.

Isaac had to keep reminding himself of that fact. He was her guardian right now, but not her Daddy. As much as his eyes were being drawn to her curves in that tight outfit, this was not about sex. No matter what his dick kept telling him.

"You'll also find a list of rules on the countertop," said Isaac. "Rules about the dog, but rules about your behavior too."

Peach arched her eyebrows at him. "What kind of rules?"

"No parties. No guests without asking my permission. You'll get up at seven and be in bed by ten. You'll tidy up after yourself."

"I thought I had a cleaner?"

"The cleaner's job is to clean, not tidy up after you," said Isaac.

"Hmmph," said Peach, sticking out her bottom lip.

That wasn't a good sign. Was she a messy Little? Isaac hated it when things weren't in their rightful place.

"Those aren't the only rules," said Isaac. "I want you to make sure you exercise for at least an hour every day, and that you spend at least two hours in Little Space."

Peach frowned. "Why? What does that matter to you?"

Isaac gave her a stern look. "My house, my rules, young lady. I won't have a Little coming to stay on my turf and neglecting her basic needs."

Peach burst out laughing. "Gosh, you really are a Daddy."

Isaac felt his spine stiffen. "Yes. Well. Those are the rules."

"And if I break them?" Peach asked.

He could have sworn she just wiggled her butt at him, but surely she wouldn't do that. He wasn't going to spank her. That would be crossing a line. He'd have to deliver other punishments. Less intimate ones. He tried to stop looking at her definitely-not-wiggling butt.

"You'll find out if you break the rules," he said, trying to focus. "Although my advice would be not to break them in the first place." He reached into his pocket. "Here. One last thing."

He handed Peach a contract. She looked at it like it was a snake about to bite her.

"It's alright," he said. "It's there to protect you."

Peach took the paperwork and Isaac noticed that her hands were shaking. "It feels so real all of a sudden."

"It's as real as our marriage is fake," he replied. He pointed at the paper. "I just need you to sign here, saying that you agree to marry me. That we won't engage in sexual intercourse so we can get the marriage annulled. And that I'll give you ten million dollars. Five once we're married. Five once we're divorced."

"Ten million," Peach echoed, as if in a trance. "I don't even... I can't..."

"That *is* what we agreed, isn't it?" said Isaac. He hoped she wasn't trying to squeeze him for more money. His offer was more than generous.

"No, yes, it's just... I think, honestly, this is all too much," Peach said. "The house, the personal shopper, and all of this stuff. I really don't need half as much as you're giving me. I feel bad."

Isaac narrowed his eyes at her. "We're going to have to work on that," he said. "I'll add a therapist to your list of staff."

"No, please!" said Peach. "Stop giving me extra stuff! It's too much!"

Isaac shook his head. "Business is business, kiddo. Take what I'm offering or the deal's off."

Peach cocked her head to one side. "Why are you doing all this for me?"

Because you're a Little.

Because I'm a Daddy Dom.

Because looking after your needs makes me feel good.

Isaac didn't say anything, just reached into his pocket again and pulled out something small and round and silver.

"You'd better wear this," he told her. "Make it official."

He took hold of her hand and slid the engagement ring onto her finger. A fourteen-carat princess-cut diamond sat in the center of it, its sparkle so full of promise.

"Is that thing real?" asked Peach warily.

"Of course," said Isaac. "Got to make the engagement believable."

"What if I lose it?" Peach asked.

"You won't," Isaac replied.

"Can I shower with it on?"

"Of course," replied Isaac. "In fact, I insist on it."

He tried not to picture Peach in the shower, naked except for that huge diamond. He tried... and failed.

"So... I guess we're officially engaged now," said Peach quietly.

"I guess we are," replied Isaac.

Peach looked again at the contract and then signed it with a trembling hand.

Isaac was surprised to feel his own anxiety spike too. They were really doing this. After a pause, he said: "Well. You go explore your new house. Let the dog have a look around too. Hopefully, you'll both be at home here."

"We definitely won't be at home," Peach replied, still staring at her ring. "But that's kind of the point."

*

It didn't make sense really. For years, Isaac had been the only one living on his compound. Now that there was another occupant, suddenly he felt even lonelier than usual.

As he sat looking over the beautiful waters of Biscayne Bay, the sunset making the sky a deep, blushing pink, he wondered whether Peach was doing the same thing at her place. Two of them, looking out at the same view from different houses.

Peach probably wasn't downing martinis right now, though. And she didn't have a stray kitten jumping all over her furniture either.

"Give it a rest, would you, Itchy?"

The kitten stared at him defiantly. She'd left little scratch marks over every surface of the house already. The walnut desk. The ebony handrail on the grand staircase. The rosewood floors. It had been a deliberate design choice to add all this expensive wood to the house, and within a matter of days, the kitten had made it all look like trash. It had probably caused thousands of dollars of damage already, if not more.

He was still trying to find an owner for the cat. The problem was, the local rescue centers were full and nobody he knew was in the market for a dirty, flea-bitten animal. His PA had sent him some allergy sprays and tablets, but even with all that stuff, Itchy was still making him feel, well, itchy.

Isaac took a long draft of his drink and then set it down, picking up a fishing rod cat toy instead. He shook it around and laughed as Itchy jumped for the little orange fish dangling on the end of it.

"You really are a funny cat, Itchy," he told it. "It's a shame that nobody wants you."

Obviously, giving the kitten a name hadn't been the best move. It felt like he was developing some kind of emotion toward it now. Like it was becoming a family member. But that was probably just all in his head. Itchy was a *cat*, after all. And he was allergic to cats. That would never change. Would it?

He looked back out at the calm waters of the bay.

Nobody wants you.

It had felt so good giving Peach her tour earlier. Slipping that ring on her finger. Telling her about his rules. He couldn't help fantasizing about what a *real* engagement might feel like if he ever found the right woman. How wonderful it would be to do all those things with his future life partner.

But what if nobody wanted to be with him forever?

For so long, Isaac had buried himself in his work. He wasn't well practiced at romance or love. Would it ever happen for him? Would anybody ever want him?

He tried to think of himself as a commodity for sale. Being a businessman, that's kinda how he thought about everything. Forty-one-year-old man for sale. Offering financial independence and a life of luxury. Looking for a Little who's not *too* Little. Who can put up with the fact her future husband sees everything in financial terms. Who struggles to show his emotions and is still torn up with grief over his dead parents. No pets.

Ha.

Not exactly the offer of the century.

Isaac put down the toy and went over to his shelves, opening up a box he almost never looked at. The box contained old photographs, mostly from when he was a boy.

He took the box back over to his armchair, then he began rifling through the pictures. There was one of his mom and dad's wedding day, three years before he was born. They looked so young and happy. His mom was wearing this ridiculously frilly white dress. His dad's arms were wrapped protectively around his mother's waist, pulling her in close to him. You could see how in love with each other they were.

And then there was a photograph of the funeral. His family, all dressed in black. Not a single smile, but no tears either. Looked like everyone was all cried out. He wasn't in the photograph because he was just a boy. Everyone said he was too young to go. It would have just upset him. But it wasn't the funeral that would have upset him, of course. It was the fact his parents weren't around anymore. At least if he'd have gone to the funeral he might have been able to process that a little better.

He'd never looked at this photo for too long before. It was too painful. He didn't get why anyone would take a photo at a funeral anyway. Seemed morbid. But now that he studied the picture, he was shocked by how bad his Aunt Meg looked in the photograph. For someone who wasn't that close to her brother, she looked sick to the stomach. He always thought she'd have been rubbing her hands together in glee knowing she was about to inherit the ranch.

Ah well. It was all in the past now.

He'd never know that much about his parents' death.

Just like he'd never know that much about true love.

Chapter Eight

PEACH

"I KNOW I SHOULDN'T..." Peach said under her breath. "But... just one more time..."

Peach was having the time of her life. Ever since she'd discovered that her house had an elevator in it, she'd been setting up dumb challenges for herself. Try to race the elevator downstairs to see who got there first. Try to do a handstand in the elevator. Try to sing "Twinkle Twinkle Little Star" in its entirety before the elevator got to the bottom.

She put Teddy down at the top of the stairs that ran to the elevator.

"Three, two, one, go!" she shouted to Teddy.

She pushed the green button on the elevator just as Teddy started to run down. This was their third race, and so far, she'd lost them all. Maybe Teddy would be tired now so she'd win, but she doubted it. That animal was full of energy.

As the elevator doors pinged open, she looked out hopefully. And then Teddy jumped at her, knocking her off her feet with shock. They both lay on the floor, happily panting.

"Teddy," she said. "This is it. We hit the big time."

Teddy licked her face. His mouth smelled of the new expensive dog food that Isaac had stocked up on for her.

"Ew," she said. "You'll put me off my second breakfast, doggy."

It was still early — Peach always woke up stoopid early. This morning it was even earlier because she was so excited to get up and explore
all the rooms again. She'd eaten ice-cream for breakfast at five a.m. Her
personal chef wasn't due to come and make her actual breakfast until
seven-thirty, which meant she had time for at least one more unofficial
breakfast before the official one.

She went over to the freezer, getting the tub of ice-cream back out.

It really was amazing how Isaac had thought of every last thing.
Especially since he had, like, no advance warning to sort it all out.
Clearly, the man had connections, and a whole team of staff buzzing
around to serve him.

As well as filling the kitchen with a range of both healthy and
unhealthy foods, Isaac had prepared a doggy room for Teddy, full of
squeaky toys and snacks and even an obstacle course for him to play
on. Then there was a playroom for Peach, full of games that could be
played by just one person. Solitaire. Hopscotch. Puzzle books. Giant
Jenga. There was the swimming pool with its own swim-up bar, hand-
ily stocked with cartons of milkshake, and there was a movie room
with a projector on the wall that played the Disney channel. It. Was.
Heaven.

She sat at the kitchen island eating ice-cream straight out of the tub,
re-reading the rules Isaac had left out for her.

No parties.

No guests without asking my permission.

Get up at seven and be in bed by ten.

Tidy up after yourself.

Eat a balanced diet.

Exercise for at least an hour every day.

Spend at least two hours in Little Space every day.

She'd never been given rules by anyone other than an employer before. It felt quite exciting to have them. She felt like she was smashing them already. She was up by five, so two hours earlier than he'd told her, which had to be a good thing, right? And she'd played at racing the elevator for the last hour, and that felt like the best exercise she'd had in years.

Okay, so she hadn't tidied up *every little thing* she'd strewn around the place, but it was impossible to stay completely tidy every single day, wasn't it? She'd probably just keep on top of the big ticket items on weekdays and then do a big tidy-up for all the itty-bitty things at the weekends.

She looked again at the rules. She didn't remember Isaac telling her about the balanced diet rule yesterday, but that wasn't going to be a problem if she had her own personal chef. She ate another big spoonful of ice-cream. Isaac wouldn't have put all this ice-cream in the freezer if he hadn't wanted her to eat it, would he?

Next to the rules, there was a detailed schedule for the next week. After the chef came to prepare her breakfast, her personal shopper was coming to pay her a visit to talk through the wedding outfit. She felt like a celebrity. Like Kim Kardashian. If Kim Kardashian was a Little. And if Kim Kardashian was into elevator races with a partially blind doggy.

"This is the life," she said aloud, with a sigh.

As much as she was enjoying herself, there was a guilty feeling nagging away inside her. It felt really strange to be having all this fun without her friends. She hadn't told them anything about this secret fake wedding plan, either. They didn't even know she was in Miami right now — they thought she'd gone back to Connecticut!

Thing was, though, she felt snubbed by them. It felt kinda good to do this without their knowledge. Maybe that's why she was eating so much ice-cream now. Trying to hide the guilt under layers of vanilla and choc chip, and cookie dough.

She shoveled in another huge spoonful and immediately regretted it.

Brain freeze!

She jumped off the chair she was perched on, and started hopping from foot to foot.

"Argh! Argh!!" she shouted. She opened her mouth as wide as it would go, trying to let some of the coldness escape from her tongue. Her temples felt like they were stuck in a vice. Her nose felt like it was pinched by a crocodile clip. "I'm dying!"

Just then, her front door burst open, and Isaac ran in.

"What is it?" he yelled, rushing over to her. "Are you alright?"

She spat the big dollop of ice-cream out into the palm of her hand and smiled up at him. "Er, brain freeze," she said, grinning with embarrassment. Her head still hurt.

Isaac looked at her, and she became aware of how she must have appeared to him.

She was still wearing her pajamas — a pink shorts and t-shirt set, with Skye from PAW Patrol on them. She was holding partially-melted, sticky ice-cream in the palm of her hand, and there were Giant Jenga blocks all over the kitchen floor.

"I see," said Isaac. "Well, I'm sorry for bursting in like that. I was about to knock, but then I heard you screaming and used my spare key."

"That's okay," said Peach. "I, er, I'm just gonna go wash this..."

Awkwardly, she stepped over the huge Jenga blocks to get to the sink and washed her hand. It was sad seeing all that good ice-cream go to waste, but there was plenty more where it had come from. At least her nose didn't feel like it was being pinched anymore.

"I came to tell you I'm heading to work shortly, and I wanted to check you were settling in okay. You found everything you need?"

"Mmm-hmm," said Peach. "It's perfect, thank you."

"Good. I'm going to be picking the wedding venue today, by the way. Any preferences?"

"Nope," said Peach, awkwardly trying to pull her shorts down over her butt. These things were so short and kept riding up between her cheeks.

"Fine," Isaac replied. "I'll just pick something straightforward then."

There was something oddly attractive about how wooden Isaac was. He seemed so stiff, like it was so hard for him to express any true emotion. It made Peach think of Mr. Darcy, in a good way.

Isaac started to go. "Just one more thing," he said, turning to her.

"Yes, sir?" asked Peach.

"Looks like you broke at least two of my rules already, so you'll receive a punishment today."

"Already? But I didn't do anything wrong! Did I?" She looked around at the Giant Jenga pieces, which she'd brought out here to try to build a new obstacle course for Teddy. And at the ice-cream melting in a sticky puddle on the countertop. And at the elevator, whose doors were currently jammed open with a stuffie and it was quietly beeping a warning at her.

Alright. Well, maybe she hadn't been perfect. But she would be from now on. Because she definitely didn't want any punishments. Definitely, *definitely* not.

*

"No, Teddy," said Peach. "I'm not breaking any more rules. We're not allowed to take you outside, remember. Not unless it's in that courtyard."

Peach pointed at the central courtyard to show Teddy where he was allowed. It's not like Teddy didn't like it in the house. They'd played with the obstacle course loads already, and Teddy had run in circles around the olive tree in the courtyard like he was a young pup again.

The problem was... he hadn't pooped.

Normally, Teddy would have done at least two poops by now, but Peach got the feeling that he couldn't go unless he was properly outside. As nice as the inner courtyard was, it still felt like part of the house, and Teddy *never* pooped inside.

"Go on," said Peach. "Just go in the courtyard and do your business. I'll get it all cleaned up."

Teddy whined at the front door for the hundredth time.

Peach bit her lip. She looked down at her schedule, then back at Teddy. "Well, maybe if we're quick..."

The personal chef had been and gone, preparing a healthy avocado and scramble tortilla for her for breakfast, and handing her a salad to eat for her lunch. She'd cleaned her teeth, as Isaac had advised, and she'd gotten herself dressed in a *Little Mermaid* themed sundress she'd had since she was thirteen, and she had a full twenty minutes left to herself before her personal shopper was due to arrive.

Fine. It wouldn't take Teddy long to go out and poop, then she'd pick it up, hide the evidence, and nobody would be any the wiser.

She opened the front door and took Teddy outside. Immediately, he bolted toward the back of Isaac's mansion and ran onto his back patio. There was a hedge between her patio and his, so Peach couldn't get to it.

"Come back here!" Peach shouted. "Teddy! That's not our place!"

Teddy looked up at her, and he looked deep into her eyes as he squirted out the runniest poop in the history of runny poops.

"Oh no," Peach said aghast. "Not good."

She wondered how the heck she was meant to clean that up. For starters, she couldn't get to it without trying to climb over or under the hedge, and on top of that, the poop was about eighty-percent liquid.

"Must be all that fancy doggy food you've been eating," said Peach. "Your tummy's not used to it yet."

Teddy ran back over to her, wagging his tail happily. Evidently, he thought he'd just done something very, very good.

"Maybe it'll rain..." she said, looking over at the brown puddle. "Or maybe if I get a bucket of water, and I throw it..."

"Ms. Trimble?" called a female voice from over by the house. "Is that you?"

Peach swallowed. Yikes. The personal shopper was here early.

"Yeah!" she called back. "I'll be one sec!"

An extremely fashionable woman in a red catsuit appeared before Peach, with a look of disdain on her face. "Oh dear," she said. "Looks like I have my work cut out for me."

Peach swallowed. "You do?"

"Darling," said the woman. "Don't you worry about a thing. We'll get you measured up and you'll never have to wear clothes that don't fit you again."

"Er... that's great," said Peach with uncertainty.

She walked back to the house with Teddy and her personal shopper, and pretty soon, all thoughts of cleaning up runny dog poop had flown out of her head.

Chapter Nine

ISAAC

ISAAC HAD NEVER HAD trouble concentrating in a boardroom meeting before. But as he sat listening to Bastion lead a talk about a potential new client for Daddies Inc — which happened to be one of the most prestigious hotel companies in the world — Isaac's mind was elsewhere.

Peach Trimble.

Even her name was distracting. Peach made him think of her Peachy ass. Trimble made him think of trembling. More precisely, her trembling ass.

Man, he'd never known he was an ass man until now. He'd always had an appreciation for all parts of a woman, but it seemed that until now, he'd been focusing his attention on the wrong kind of women. The perfectly put-together, skinny Littles in expensive cropped t-shirts to show off their flat midriffs. Littles whose bodies were as lithe as teenagers, who lived the lifestyle so perfectly it was like they were made for Instagram.

He wasn't into the bratty types, either. He always went for Little princesses, who never acted up, just quietly colored in or chilled out in Little Space while he got on with whatever he had to do. No trouble. No fuss.

Not so with Peach Trimble.

Peach Trimble was a messy, chaotic, wobbly, bouncy, unpredictable, hurricane of a woman. Her Littleness vibrated in every cell of her voluptuous body. She represented all the parts of life that Isaac had tried to eradicate from himself over the years. Untidiness, laziness, silliness.

That's partly the reason he thought marrying her was a safe bet. He wasn't going to fall for her. Things wouldn't get messy. But although his common sense was clear on that, his dick had other ideas. The moment she bent down to talk to her ratty little pup this morning, and he'd seen a glimpse of that curvaceous ass and those mint green panties, his cock had hardened to full thickness.

There was something magnetic about Peach Trimble. Not in spite of her chaos, but *because* of it. Spending time with her helped Isaac remember happier times. Times when he didn't obsess over bank balances, schedules, and manners. Times when he was growing up on the ranch, happy and free. Where every day was a blank slate, ready to be scribbled on in all the glorious colors of the rainbow.

"You got a problem with something I'm saying?" said Bastion, breaking off from his speech and turning to him.

Isaac raised his palms. "No, man," he said. "You've done great. Sounds like a good deal."

He meant it too. Bastion's work had been sloppy ever since his divorce. This new deal with the hotel chain was his saving grace. It was clear that he was back in Montague's good books. And Bastion seemed to be standing a little taller today, too. He'd even shaved for the first time in weeks. He wondered what had brought about the change in him. Was it just the hotel deal? Or did Bastion have his eye on a Little too?

"Thought you were drifting off for a minute there," said Bastion. "And then you started smirking, so I assumed—"

"It's all good, man," said Isaac. "I don't have a problem with any of it."

There was an uncomfortable silence in the room. Montague looked at both men questioningly, and Sam, the head of Human Resources cleared his throat.

"Shall we continue?" Sam asked.

Bastion shrugged. "Sure."

Isaac tried to stay focused this time, but he was only about three seconds in when he found himself thinking about her again. About how cute she looked in his place. In those tight PJs. Ice-cream running down her chin. Those big blue eyes. Those chubby cheeks. That petite but curvaceous figure.

He could feel his cock hardening again right now, here in the board-room. He longed to stroke it, to rub himself hard while thinking about *her*. He longed to stick it between those ample ass cheeks and come harder than he'd ever come in his life.

Trying not to draw any attention to himself, he rested his hand on the top of his pant leg, right where his thick cock lay, hot and hard and heavy, desperate to shoot its load.

Mmmm, that felt good...

He thought about her mouth, dribbling ice-cream. He thought about her fleshy buttocks. He thought about the punishment he would be doling out to her later...

He'd never been one of those Daddies who got off on endlessly punishing their Little. He didn't have time to think up a million and one punishments. He normally just role-played a spanking session with his Littles every now and then. The scene would be laid out in great detail, and both parties would know exactly what to expect. The implement to be used. The number of strikes. The situation they'd be acting out. They'd sign an agreement saying they'd stick to the script. Isaac had always enjoyed the precision of it.

When he'd knocked on Peach's door this morning, though, he'd found himself *hoping* she'd have done something naughty. He'd spent the night fantasizing about all the delicious ways he might torment her for being a bad girl on his premises. He'd jerked off thinking about her sulky pout as he inflicted all kinds of tasty torture on her.

The moment he saw that she'd broken his rules, he'd gotten excited. It was plain to see that she hadn't tidied up after herself, and given how much ice-cream she'd shoveled into her pretty mouth, she wasn't eating a balanced diet, either. He could also see from his Smartphone app that she had been up at five. The app told him how much energy each of his appliances were using, and for some reason, it looked like she'd been using the elevator almost constantly for the first hour.

In any case, she deserved the punishment he was dishing out to her. And by the time he got home tonight, the punishment would be in full swing.

He pressed down a little harder on his hungry cock, rubbing it just the tiniest bit. He'd never done something like this before. Bastion was the one who jerked off pretty much anywhere, and boasted about it too. The man was a walking cum factory. Isaac had never let himself get turned on during office hours.

Unable to help himself, a small moan escaped his lips.

"Seriously, dude?" said Bastion. "You sure you're okay with this deal? You're making funny noises now."

Isaac swallowed. "Sorry. Got a lot on my mind."

A whole lot of Peach Trimble.

"It's alright," Montague cut in. "I'm kinda distracted too. Got so much to sort out for the wedding. Daisy and I have been chatting about it almost constantly for three weeks now." He turned to Bastion. "You've done good, man. Real good. How about we all go to Dade-D Bar to celebrate?"

"You mean... take the afternoon off?" asked Isaac. They never did that. It was like an unwritten rule.

"Yeah," said Montague. "Feels like we could all do with letting off a little steam. Plus, the three of us haven't hung in, like, forever."

Sam, the HR guy, pouted. "Guess I'm not invited then."

"Sorry, dude," said Montague. "This is one of the perks of being a business owner. But the three of us will be back in tomorrow, bright-eyed and bushy-tailed."

"You'd better be," Sam huffed.

Bastion turned off the projector and clapped his hands together. "I'm so up for this!" he said. "I've got a thirst for whiskey sours."

"You always do," joked Montague.

Isaac tried to push his cock discreetly between his legs as he stood up, getting ready to go.

*

Three glasses clinked together. Three old friends said "Cheers" and clapped each other on the back.

Things had changed since the last time they'd done this, though. Montague was getting married — again. Clearly, he was with his Forever Girl now, though. Daisy was a keeper, and it was great to see how happy they were together, but it felt like Isaac had lost his best friend in the process.

Bastion was recently divorced. His ex-wife, Clarabelle, had decided that she wasn't a Little, after all. Never really acted like one anyway, other than the fact she always wore pink. She was actually older than Bastion — almost fifty now — and she'd decided last year that she wanted a toyboy, and ran off with a twenty-five-year-old stripper named Gav. Last time Bastion heard from her, she was pregnant with Gav's triplets and they were running some pregnancy fetish website together somewhere.

And now, Isaac was due to get married, but the relationship was fake, and his best pals knew nothing about it.

"So... are you going to tell us where this mystery wedding venue is yet?" asked Isaac, taking a sip of his martini.

" Nope," replied Montague without skipping a beat, "but I think you'll be surprised."

"I hate secrets," said Bastion, downing his first whiskey sour and moving onto the second, which he'd ordered himself at the same time as the first. "Secrets lead to lies, and lies lead to your wife running off with a young gigolo."

Isaac cast Bastion a sympathetic look, but he felt a sting of guilt in his stomach. "Speaking of secrets," he said, taking a deep breath. "I have some news."

Bastion and Montague both looked at him with nervous eyes. Normally, when Isaac said that he had news, that meant he was about to tell them they owed money or they'd made money.

"It's personal news, actually," he continued. "It turns out..." He tried to keep his cool. Tried to make this seem perfectly natural. "Turns out I'm getting married myself."

Montague and Bastion looked as shocked and confused as Isaac had expected.

"What?!" asked Bastion.

"To who?" asked Montague.

"Well, you actually know her," said Isaac.

This was so hard. He'd been dreading this moment. He hadn't planned on revealing the wedding to his friends today, but he needed to make it seem as real as possible. This was exactly the kind of setting he'd reveal something like this if it was real, so he had to make the most of the moment.

"You'd better not be marrying Clarabelle," spat Bastion. "Or I'll punch you in the head."

"Not Clarabelle," said Isaac quickly. "She's someone we only recently met, actually."

"How recently?" asked Montague, raising an eyebrow.

"A couple days ago," said Isaac with a casual shrug.

Bastion turned pale. "It's one of Daisy's friends, isn't it?"

Isaac nodded, and then cast Montague a sincere look. It wasn't easy to be fake-marrying his best friend's fiancée.

"I knew it," said Bastion, his cheeks flushed. "Well, Kiera's hot as hell, so it makes sense." He gritted his teeth. "Didn't think you were her type, though. Plus, she's kind of a punk. She'd eat you alive. And I'm sure she's nothing but trouble."

Why was Bastion getting so worked up about the idea of him marrying Kiera? Was he into her?

"It's not Kiera," Isaac said. "It's... the other one." He couldn't bring himself to say her name out loud. He was worried that just having her name on his lips would give him another hard-on.

"You're marrying Peach?" asked Montague incredulously. "Daisy told me she hates you."

"It's... a love-hate kind of a thing," Isaac said awkwardly.

Bastion grunted and downed his second whiskey sour.

"You yelled at her for bringing a dog into the office," said Montague. "How did you go from *that* to wedding bells?"

"It's complicated," said Isaac, relieved that at least that part wasn't a lie. "But she's moved in with me now. And you can expect wedding invitations by the end of the week."

"By the end of the *week*?" exclaimed Montague. "You're gonna get your invitations out before mine!"

Isaac frowned. "Not a competition, is it?"

Montague narrowed his eyes at him. "Dude, you're making a big mistake. You can't have fallen for her that fast. She's using you for your money."

He's right, thought Isaac. *But I'm using her for the marriage certificate.*

"Keep the weekend free," said Isaac.

"*This* weekend?" said Montague incredulously. "Your wedding will be before mine?"

"Not. A. Competition," replied Bastion moodily.

The mood had changed between them all now. Isaac felt like crap. He wanted so badly to tell his friends the truth. They knew all about his family ranch, and how his aunt had inherited it instead of him. They'd have understood why he had put the plan in action...

But they'd be mad at him too. Marrying a Little on false pretenses. Involving her in his deceitful plan. Risking her happiness for his own. They'd have talked him out of the plan in ten minutes flat.

Thing is, they didn't know Peach. They didn't see her crying the other day. They didn't know how much money he was giving her, and how much it could change her life. They didn't know how much he respected her. That he felt responsible for her happiness above all else. That it would be his mission to make this deal go smoothly for her sake as much as for his own.

"Listen," said Isaac. "I know it's a big ask, but I'd like you to keep this between us for now." He shot a look at Montague.

"Not a chance," said Montague. "I'm not lying to my babygirl."

"I'm not asking you to lie to Daisy," said Isaac. "Just... don't tell her yet. Peach and I want to keep it to ourselves for now. It's all been so fast, such a whirlwind. I've already said too much. Just give us a couple days."

"You're a damn fool," said Bastion under his breath. "She's taking you for a ride."

"Peach deserves more than this," Montague grumbled.

Isaac smiled at them both, trying to deflate the tension. "How about I get us another round of drinks? I'd really like to celebrate with you guys. Trust me, this is a good thing."

Bastion didn't look up, but nodded grumpily.

Montague stared into Isaac's eyes, as though trying to warn him of something.

Isaac shot over to the bar, relieved to step away from the bad vibes at the table for a moment. He knew that breaking his news was going to go down like a lead balloon, but it was an even worse reception than he'd expected. He should have prepared his friends first. Told them he was taking Peach on a date today. That he'd kissed her tomorrow. That he'd proposed to her the day after that.

Nah, who was he kidding? However he'd played it this week, his friends would have been shocked. It was all being done in a big rush, and it didn't make any sense. Well, it didn't make any sense to *them*. But Isaac had his eyes on the prize. This time next week, he'd have told his aunt the wonderful news: that he was married and eligible to take the family ranch off her hands.

As Cindy poured the drinks, Isaac ran his eyes over the names of all the crazy freakshakes they sold here for the Littles. It was cool that Daddies Inc had set up this bar. That there was a safe social space for Daddies and Littles to hang out, and something here for everyone.

To the left of the bar there was a pool table for the Daddies, and on the other side, there was a selection of board games for the Littles. He needed to find somewhere like this for the wedding. Somewhere that catered for everyone.

Unless... wait a minute. This place was perfect. It would be so simple to arrange. In fact, he could do it right now.

"Say, Cindy?" said Isaac. "Do you ever do weddings here?"

Cindy put down her cocktail shaker and smiled. "As a matter of fact," she said, "we do."

"How does this weekend sound? Think you could fit me in?"

Cindy looked taken aback. "This weekend? Well, I didn't know this place was so popular. And it's not much notice. But I'd do anything for you guys, so..." She shrugged. "Sure. Why not?"

A warm thrill of excitement ran through Isaac. "Good," he said. "Then it's settled."

By the weekend, he'd be married.

To the girl with the peachy ass.

Chapter Ten

PEACH

T OTAL WHIRLWIND. THAT WAS the only way to describe it.

The personal shopper had come to take her measurements for a wedding dress — plus a whole new wardrobe. They'd flicked through hundreds, maybe thousands, of images: tops, bottoms, pinafores, overalls, onesies, pajamas — and Peach had to say "yes" or "no" to each of them. It was like Tinder for outfits. Even Teddy got measured up for a wedding suit, as well as a few doggy costumes.

As soon as the personal shopper left, the personal *trainer* arrived. Apparently, all the running up and down the stairs to race the elevator this morning didn't count as real exercise, so he made her do twenty minutes of cardio, twenty of strength, and then a twenty-minute swim in the pool.

After that came the masseuse, who had done something involving warm stones on her spine that felt very nice indeed, especially after all that yucky exercise.

Then lunch. Then a full check-over with her doctor, who took blood, checked her vitals, and even gave her some birth control pills. Then a meeting with her financial adviser, who helped her set up a number of high-interest easy-access bank accounts to put her first million into. Finally, the life coach, who took one look at her and said she needed to rest today and that she'd be back tomorrow.

It had been *a lot*. But it also felt kind of amazing. She was being treated like royalty. All this free stuff. All this attention. Obviously, it *wasn't* romance. She barely knew her partner and had never even kissed him. Never would. But she had to admit, she had felt a glow of pride when the private chef told her what a great boss Isaac was — giving him days off for family events and self-care — and the life coach mentioned that he even paid for her healthcare.

It was odd, but Peach had found herself growing more impatient to see Isaac again as the day went on. She wanted to tell him how nice everyone had been, and how grateful she was for all this stuff. He wasn't due back for another hour, though, and in the meantime, she had a mystery to solve.

All day long there had been a package sitting on the kitchen countertop. The personal shopper had brought it with her this morning, and had instructed her to open it only when all of her meetings for the day had finished.

The package was a white box wrapped in a pink ribbon, and there was a gift tag attached to it. Peach hadn't had a chance to read the tag yet, but now, she approached it with caution. Isaac had given her so much already. What could he possibly be giving her on top of all that other stuff?

She looked at the plain white tag, and read the two words on the back, written in black Sharpie.

YOUR PUNISHMENT.

Oh, my. There was some kind of punishment in here? She untied the ribbon and took off the lid of the box, her hands trembling. Inside, there was something that looked like a towel.

Eh?

She started pulling it out and realized that it wasn't a towel at all. It was simply made of soft terrycloth. It was a white onesie with a hood, and across the front were some words stitched in baby pink.

"I'VE BEEN A BAD BUNNY."

There was a note inside the box too.

Babygirl,

Here's your punishment for breaking some of our rules this morning. Wear this until I get back. Stand in the naughty corner while you wear it. That's the corner of the kitchen opposite the refrigerator. Put your hands on the wall and stick your butt in the air. Then wait.

Isaac

What the...? This was unlike any punishment Peach had fantasized about before. Wear a onesie? In the naughty corner?

She took off her clothes, throwing them down onto the kitchen floor in a messy pile, then she pulled on the onesie. It felt good against her skin. Soft and snuggly. Not much of a punishment, to be honest. As she explored the outfit, she noticed that there was a fluffy white tail on the butt, and that the entire section over her bottom could be lifted down like a flap. Was that there in case she needed to pee?

She lifted up the hood, noticing the long, floppy bunny ears stuck to it, and then she looked over at the naughty corner.

This felt so weird.

She got an urge to call Daisy or Kiera, to tell them all about it and ask them if she should go along with this weird stuff Isaac was telling her to do. But she still couldn't bring herself to talk to them. They'd abandoned her, so she was abandoning *them*.

She looked at Teddy, who blinked up at her, perfectly oblivious to how strange this situation was.

Then, she padded over to the naughty corner, and she placed her palms on the wall.

Well.

This was... different.

According to the schedule, there were still forty-five minutes until Isaac was due back. That's because the life coach had seen how tired she was and left her to get some rest. This didn't count as rest, though, did it? Standing still was actually quite hard work. She wanted to sit down — or better still, lie down — and watch cartoons until the sun set.

She leaned forward and yawned, her bunny ears flopping over as she did so.

"This sucks," she sighed. "I've been such a good girl today as well, Teddy. I even ate those green things in the salad at lunchtime."

She did too. She ate all the things of all the colors because the exercise made her so hungry.

Suddenly, she heard a knock at the door, and then a key turning.

"This is a pleasant surprise," said a familiar deep voice. "I'm early, but you're already waiting for me."

Peach felt a swell of pride. "I'm being a good girl today."

She kept her eyes on the wall and could hear Isaac's voice growing louder as he got closer. "I don't know about that," he said. "Your clothes are strewn all over the floor. And there's still the matter of those rules you broke this morning."

Peach bit her lip. "Yes, that's true. But I promise I won't do it again, Daddy."

Oh crap, where had that word come from? Isaac wasn't her Daddy, just like he wasn't her boyfriend.

"Good girl for calling me Daddy," said Isaac, right behind her now, running his hands over the soft fabric of the onesie, his hands traveling down her spine.

"I thought you hated animals, Daddy," Peach said, her voice strangely hoarse. "But here I am, dressed up as one for you."

"I don't hate animals," said Isaac. "I just think they ought to stay in their place."

"And what place is that?" asked Peach, sticking her butt out in the air like the note had advised her to do.

"The naughty corner, of course," replied Isaac, his hands on her butt now, his breath becoming faster. Then, she felt his fingers unfastening the velcro of the butt flap on the onesie, and she felt the cool air on her panties. She felt relieved she was wearing her very best pair: lilac ones with a lacy trim.

"Oh dear," said Isaac. "Looks like my babygirl is going to need some new panties. These ones are a disgrace."

Humph. That didn't feel good. These ones were only a year old. And they didn't even come in a multipack like some of her others.

Isaac ran his hands over her panties now, causing her butt to clench involuntarily.

"Sshhh, babygirl," he said. "Relax those muscles. This'll be much more bearable for you if you can relax."

"What will?" asked Peach, confused.

"Address me as 'Daddy' or 'sir'," snapped Isaac.

"Oh, sorry, Daddy. What are you about to do to me, Daddy, sir?"

"I'm about to show you what a bad bunny you've been," said Isaac, pinching the flesh of her butt. She'd always been a little embarrassed by her bum. She was curvy all over, but her bum felt disproportionately big. She was definitely pear-shaped. Somehow, her weight just seemed to sit around her hips and butt, no matter what.

"You have no idea," Isaac said, pressing his weight against her and growling into her ear, "what this ass of yours has been doing to me. How much it's been tormenting me today."

"It has, Daddy?" asked Peach, feeling her pussy begin to bloom with moisture.

"It's a very naughty, very flirty little bottom," Isaac told her. "And it's going to bear the brunt of this punishment."

Peach swallowed.

"Five spanks over your panties," Isaac told her. "And then five spanks without them."

Without them?

In spite of herself, Peach felt herself becoming very, very wet. This was definitely the weirdest situation she'd ever been in, but it was making her hot as the sun.

"If it hurts too much," he told her, "just bark like a dog and I'll stop."

"Bark like a dog, sir?"

"That's right," he replied. "Like the animal you are, Peach Trimble."

Peach nodded. "Alright, Daddy." She didn't like the thought of barking like a dog in front of Isaac, but she was pretty sure she wouldn't have to. She could take any amount of pain he wanted to dish out to her. And she wouldn't just take it. She'd enjoy it.

Isaac's hand stroked her panties one more time, and then there was a moment when nothing happened. She almost said something, but then she felt the full force of his palm smacking down on her.

Ooof.

She'd always *imagined* that she was good with pain, but nobody had ever spanked her in real life. She'd done tests on herself and concluded that she had a high pain threshold, but being hit by someone else — someone much stronger than her — was a different thing altogether.

Isaac wasn't holding back, and she expected that she'd have a bruised ass by tomorrow.

More smacks, and Peach felt the pain radiate through her wobbling bottom each time.

Finally, Isaac reached the fifth smack, and then she felt his fingers tucking under the lacy waistband of her panties. Slowly, he pulled them down, and she felt her ass being exposed to him bit by bit. Would he find her cellulite a turn-off? Her butt was fat and dimply and rippled every time it was touched. Was he really ready to see this?

"Damn, Ms. Trimble," said Isaac breathlessly. "You have the Sistine Chapel of asses."

"What does that mean, sir?" Peach asked quietly.

"It means you have the most exquisite ass in the whole damn world. A man could lose his cock in that thing for hours at a time."

Peach's eyes widened in shock. "You like to do that?"

"Right now, babygirl," Isaac said gruffly, "it's the *only* thing I want to do."

Peach lifted her ass a little higher. "Well, maybe we could do that instead of...?"

She had never been entered anally before, but it couldn't hurt worse than a spanking, could it? Besides, she was feeling so hot and bothered right now, she felt like she would agree to do anything Isaac wanted.

"Not a chance," Isaac replied.

She felt his hand smack down on her ass. Without the constraints of panties, she felt her flesh jiggle and wobble and ripple for a long time afterward. Isaac didn't say anything, and she worried that he'd been put off by the sight of it.

"Daddy?" she whispered. "Please don't stop."

"Stay still," Isaac urged her, pushing her up harder against the wall.

She managed to cast a quick look behind her, and she noticed that he had freed his cock from his pants, and he was jerking off while staring intently at her butt. She couldn't believe how long and thick his cock was. How hard he was for her even though she was dressed in this silly onesie.

"Stick your butt up higher for me," he ordered her.

She did as she was told, and almost instantly, she felt Isaac's warm cum spill across her backside. She even felt a dollop of it trickle down to her asshole.

"Good," he said, his voice sounding strained. "I can focus again now."

With that, he gave her the four remaining smacks, spreading his cum all over his hand and her bottom cheeks, and then he pulled up her panties, pulled down the flap of the onesie, and turned her to face him.

He looked surprisingly put together. His cock was hidden away back in his pants, and she almost wondered if the whole thing had been a dream. Maybe she would have thought it was, if it hadn't been for the fact that she could still feel his cum dribbling into her asshole.

"Now, babygirl," he said. "I have a surprise for you."

"Another one?"

He smiled.

*

"You haven't seen a real sunset until you've seen a sunset over Biscayne Bay," Isaac told her as he pulled out a chair for her.

He had asked his chef to prepare dinner for them out on his deck. Silver domes sat over the plates, and Peach wondered what was going to be under them: warm salad, cold salad, or a mixture of the two?

Peach pulled down her sundress, which barely covered her butt. Isaac had let her change out of the bunny onesie since she was no longer being a bad girl, but he'd ordered her to keep the same cum-soaked panties on. Her sundress, which was another she'd had since she was a teenager, was much too short on her, barely covering her ass, and she felt nervous in it all of a sudden.

"You seem self-conscious around me," Isaac observed as they both sat. "Like you're embarrassed of your body."

Peach smiled nervously. "Well... I am... a bit."

Isaac frowned. "But why?"

"Well, let's just say I'm not like all the models you see in magazines."

"No, you're not," said Isaac. "And thank god for that. Your body is *real*, Peach Trimble. Your body makes a man feel like a man."

"Thanks... I think," said Peach.

"Seriously," he said. "If I wasn't doing this whole fake marriage thing with you, then I'd—" Isaac stopped himself partway through the sentence.

"You'd what, sir?" asked Peach.

"Well, I'd do more than empty my balls on your ass, babygirl." Isaac looked embarrassed as he said that. An admission that it had really happened.

"So... we can't do more than that?" Peach asked awkwardly.

"Not unless we want to get ourselves into a giant mess," Isaac replied. "Once this marriage is over, the quickest way to make it go away is with an annulment. And if we fuck, we're screwed."

"I see," said Peach. It's not like she entered into this agreement wanting to have sex with Isaac, but she'd gone on a whole rollercoaster of emotions today, and her pussy didn't seem to want to get off the ride. "But isn't that just... once we're married? I mean, if you have sex *before* you get married that doesn't count, does it? You can still get the annulment as long as you don't have sex after—"

"Sweetheart," Isaac interrupted her. "The more times I hear you say the word 'sex', the more dangerous this thing gets for us. I can promise you now, if I was to put my cock in your pussy, even once, we'd be screwed. Because I just know how hard it would be to stop."

"Oh," said Peach, blushing. "Right."

"Anyway," said Isaac. "Dinner is served." He lifted the two big silver domes off their plates.

Peach gasped. "Steak and French fries? I thought it'd be some health food. Thought you were trying to make me into some skinny person for the wedding, with thighs of steel and a flat ass."

Isaac's eyes widened. "Fuck, no. I don't want your appearance to change. Not an inch of it. I just want to make sure I'm looking after your health and wellbeing while I'm your... guardian."

"Were you about to say Daddy?" Peach teased.

"Would you mind if I did?"

"You know I wouldn't," said Peach, biting her lip.

"We should be careful," said Isaac, suddenly serious. "The situation we're in is clearly a turn-on. The fact that it's all so forbidden. We don't want to mistake anything we're feeling as being real."

"Oh," Peach replied. "No." She bit on a French fry glumly.

"I have the wedding venue organized," said Isaac, as they ate. "The invitations are being printed tonight. I thought you might like me to come with me when we deliver them to your friends. Tomorrow, or maybe the day after?"

"It's all so fast," said Peach quietly, looking out at the pink sky and the beautiful reflections it made over the water. Another experience that *should* have been romantic, but wasn't because none of this was real.

Was his coming on her ass real? Or was it all just some kind of weird roleplay? Maybe he was getting off on the fact that this whole thing was fake. That's what he meant about the situation being a turn-on. He liked her because he didn't really like her.

"What's up, Peach?" asked Isaac, putting down his cutlery and reaching for her hand. "You having second thoughts about this?"

Peach shook her head. "No. It's just... a lot. Like, a lot of responsibility and change."

Isaac looked as though the truth had just dawned on him. "Oh, shit," he said. "This schedule I gave you. I haven't scheduled in enough time in Little Space, have I? I assumed you'd just make time for that in your free time in the evenings, but the truth is, you need that on your schedule just as much as any of the other stuff."

Peach smiled. "That's kind of you, but I don't get a lot of time in Little Space normally anyway. Not with the volunteer job, and the pet-grooming job, and looking after Teddy, and everything else. Life has been too busy, I guess."

Isaac shook his head. "This business proposition is meant to be mutually beneficial. I don't want to add to your problems. How about this? As long as you're living under my roof, I'll treat you like my Little."

Peach raised her eyebrows. "How?"

He'd already given her rules and spanked her. What more could he do?

"That involves me looking after your Little as much as possible," said Isaac. "Helping you find the time to play, coddling and nurturing you like a Daddy."

"Are you talking about sex?" asked Peach quietly, feeling her cheeks redden.

"No," he said, swallowing. "Not unless you want it. Although that would have to happen after the annulment had taken place, of course."

Peach remained silent. What she wanted to say was that she wouldn't be under his roof anymore after the annulment. But she didn't feel like saying those words right now.

"Ice-cream?" said Isaac, as the chef brought out two bowls.

"I'm allowed more ice-cream today?" said Peach, shocked. This was strawberry ice-cream, with extra strawberry sauce.

"I've been informed that you ate all your lunch. So yes. I'll allow it since this is a special occasion."

"It is?" Peach asked.

"It's not every day that I get to see the Sistine Chapel of asses," Isaac joked. "And it's not every day I get to come on it."

Peach giggled, looking over at the chef, who was thankfully walking away.

"Oh, fuck," said Isaac, staring at her.

"What?" asked Peach. "What is it?" He was staring at something on her face. As she felt around trying to figure it out, she realized that there was a big stream of ice-cream dribbling down her chin.

"You have no idea what that sight does to me," said Isaac.

"The sight of me dribbling ice-cream?" asked Peach, confused.

Peach took her hand and held it over his crotch. She could feel the warmth and girth of him immediately.

"I've never had so many hard-ons in one damn day," he said. He looked into her eyes, then down at her mouth. "Put another spoonful of ice-cream in your mouth," he ordered her. "But don't swallow it."

Amused, Peach did as she was told.

Isaac stood and walked over to her. He unzipped his fly and held his cock out to her mouth. "Suck it," he commanded.

Peach looked down at his thick, veined cock, purple-headed and desperate for her touch.

She opened her mouth, melting ice-cream dribbling down her chin and neck, and she took his cock into her.

The ice-cream was cold and his cock was hot. The combination of the two felt indescribably wonderful. Isaac slid in and out of her as melted ice-cream dripped down her throat, her breasts, into her crotch. Isaac yanked at her hair, thrusting in and out of her so deep and with such force it almost made her spit out the ice-cream. Somehow, she managed to keep going, and before she knew it, Isaac's cum was shooting down her throat along with the remainder of the melted strawberry ice-cream.

"Fuck," said Isaac. "Daddy's going to buy you an extra special stuffie tomorrow to say thank you. That was perfect."

"A new stuffie *and* some new panties?" asked Peach. She couldn't believe how much stuff Isaac kept giving her. And the truth was, it's not like any of this was a hardship for her. The spanking. The ice-cream blowjob. Even the marriage. She was having fun, and getting showered with gifts at the same time. It was win-win!

Just then, something seemed to catch his attention. He was staring down at the ground.

"Wait a sec. Is that... dog mess on my deck?"

Peach blushed. "I'm sorry, Daddy," she said, wiping her mouth with the back of her hand. She could still taste strawberries and cum, and it was hard to focus. "I tried to keep Teddy confined to the courtyard, but he needed to poop and he couldn't do it in there, so I took him outside, and before I knew it—"

"Young lady," said Isaac. "Over my knee. Now."

Chapter Eleven

ISAAC

"I'M NOT GOING TO spank this ass again today," Isaac said, examining the red handprints he'd left on the surface of her skin. "It's too soon for that. You need time to heal."

He noticed her squirming on his lap, and the thin trail of moisture trickling out of her pussy and down her inner thigh.

"Besides," he said, "something tells me that you'd enjoy a spanking too much right now."

The truth is, Isaac would enjoy it too. Even though his balls had been emptied twice this evening, he knew it was only a matter of time before he got hard again. This girl was everything his cock had ever wanted. It felt strange to admit that when she was so obviously not his type. But... what if his brain had one type, but his *balls* had another? And if that was the case, what about his heart? What was his heart's type?

Isaac reached into his pocket and pulled out a brand new butt plug, still in its packaging. He'd stopped in at a sex store on the way home and bought a whole bunch of anal play stuff. He couldn't help himself. Her thick ass had been on his mind way too much today. Plus, after the meeting with his friends had gone so badly, he'd needed to do something cheer himself up.

This plug was made of pink glass, with a white teddy bear stuck on the flat end of it. The round end was beautifully soft and glinted in the pink light of the sunset.

"What are you doing, sir?" asked Peach quietly. Her voice sounded so much smaller and younger now than when they'd first met. He enjoyed bringing out the Littleness in her, seeing how easy it was to regress her. So many women he'd dated previously had all tried to resist it, even if they swore that they were into age play. With Peach, it was like *she* was strawberry ice-cream, melting and sweet in the palm of his hand.

His cock tingled just thinking about the feeling of that ice-cream in her mouth. He needed to focus on what he was doing, or he'd get hard again right now, and he didn't want to rush this.

"I'm inserting something into you, Little girl," he said plainly. "Look."

He held the butt plug out for her to see, knowing that the sight of it would provoke a reaction in her. Immediately, she gasped.

"Is that a... Are you plugging my botty, Daddy?"

He glowed with pride when she used that name. It made him feel so manly and so caring all at once.

"Yes, sweetheart," he said. "That's exactly what I'm doing. Anyone ever done that to you before? Or did you ever do it yourself?"

"No, Daddy," said Peach. "But I trust you."

Good girl. He hadn't earned her trust fully yet, but she was willing to give it to him, and that meant a lot. He'd show her that she could count on him. They were about to get married, after all. Even if it wasn't going to last very long, it was still happening. She would be his wife soon enough.

"Alright, darling," he said. "You just lie there, nice and heavy, and take a big breath in, then a long, relaxed breath out for me."

Peach did as she was told. As she breathed in, Isaac dipped his forefinger into the moist honeypot of her pussy, then rubbed his slick finger over her asshole. It still had a little of his cum pooling inside it from earlier, which would help lubricate her even more. She quivered and clenched as he touched her, but as soon as she started to breathe out, she relaxed. Isaac took that opportunity to slide the pink glass plug deep into her back passage, and he marveled at how easily the smooth, rounded object slid into her.

Now it was in, it looked glorious. Her perfectly peachy ass, pinkened from her spanking, seemed complete with the cute plug between its cheeks. The happy little teddy bear smiled as it nestled between her buttocks and he looked at it enviously for a moment, looking forward to the moment that *he* got to slide in deep between her cheeks too.

"That feels good, Daddy," said Peach, squirming again.

"Hmmm," he said. "It's not meant to be a reward."

"Oh," said Peach quickly, "Well, obviously it feels a bit strange, like I'm being stretched open somewhere I've never been opened up before. But... I'd be lying if I said I didn't like it, Daddy."

Isaac swelled with pleasure. This *was* meant to be a punishment, but it was a very good sign that Peach was enjoying herself. That butt plug wasn't the only thing he wanted to put in her back passage. This was going to have to be a punishment of delayed gratification rather than one of inflicting pain.

"Panties up," said Isaac. "Sit down and finish your dinner."

"I can sit on that thing?" said Peach. "It won't shatter inside me?"

"No, sweetheart," said Isaac, "it won't shatter. You're perfectly safe. Just sit down slowly so you don't get a shock." He patted Peach's bottom, watching the wonderful ripples that played across the surface of her skin.

Then, she stood up, pulled up her panties, and turned to face him. Slowly, she sat back down. Isaac heard the clink of the plug as it touched the chair, and he watched Peach's eyes widen for a moment... and then a dreamy expression replaced the look of surprise.

"Does that feel good?"

"Almost too good, Daddy," replied Peach. "I can feel the plug inside me, rubbing against my... I feel like I want to... touch myself."

"Not a chance," Isaac replied. "You are not allowed to touch yourself unless I say so."

Peach bit her lip. "It's just... quite hard to... concentrate."

Isaac leaned forward. "You want more don't you?"

Peach gave him the tiniest nod.

"Is that a yes?" Isaac asked. He felt his cock begin to thicken as his voice became more commanding. He loved dominating her like this. It was such a damn turn-on.

Peach nodded again, more vigorously this time.

"Say it," Isaac urged her.

"Yes, Daddy," said Peach meekly.

"Say it louder," Isaac said.

"*Yes, Daddy!*" Peach gasped. "Yes, Daddy! I want to make myself come! I feel like I'm so close already. Or, or, I feel like I want *you* to make me come. Maybe if you just... put your hand between my legs... or even your face... and... flicked your tongue..."

Peach was panting, rubbing her ass on the chair, clearly close to coming right now.

"Oh dear," said Isaac. "This won't do at all." He put his arms around Peach's waist, wrapping her legs around him. Careful not to touch the butt plug, he placed one hand under her ass for support.

Obviously, by now he had a raging boner all over again, and he wanted nothing more than to fuck his pretty little fiancée until she screamed his name into the Miami night... but he couldn't let that happen.

"Where are we going, Daddy?" asked Peach, squirming against his crotch, rubbing her soaking wet pussy against his hard-on, threatening to make him explode in his underpants.

"To help you cool down, of course," he replied.

He carried her into his mansion, making sure to steer clear of the kitchen, where his chef was no doubt cleaning up. Thankfully, when you were as rich as Isaac was, you were able to employ a certain caliber of staff. Staff who were able to be discreet. Who knew when to look in the opposite direction, or when to leave work and come back later.

"What was that noise, Daddy?" asked Peach, suddenly stiffening.

Isaac paused. "What noise?"

"It was, like... er... *miaow*?" She squeaked out the last sound, doing her best kitten impression.

Isaac gritted his teeth together. "Nothing," he said. "You must be imagining it."

He couldn't let Peach think he was a softhearted fool. Couldn't let her think the kitten would be staying here, either. The second he found a home for that thing, it was being shipped off immediately.

"I guess I must be," said Peach. "You're not the kind of man to have a pet, Daddy."

"Damn straight," Isaac growled. "Only pet around here is *you*, my little kitten."

With that, he carried Peach upstairs and placed her down on the cold bathroom tiles while he ran a hot bath for her. Hopefully, this would distract them both for a while. Blow-jobs and butt plugs were one thing, but full-blown intercourse definitely couldn't happen between them. Not now, not ever.

*

Her body looked beautiful laced with delicate white bubbles. Shiny from the essential oils he'd put in the bath, making her smell of lavender and peppermint. Good enough to eat. It felt good to see her looking so at home here, too. Sitting in his rolltop bath, her cheeks pink from the steam, a content smile on her lips.

Every new light that he saw her in, he found himself admiring her a little bit more. Bathtime Peach was warm and pliant. Her mischievous side gave way to her innate ability to deeply relax. She was the opposite of him in just about every way. So full of fun, but able to rest and rejuvenate when needed. Isaac had only seemed to have one switch lately. The switch that made him work hard... and occasionally, work even harder.

The last couple days, though, since Peach had entered his life, he'd found some inner peace. And some excitement too. The kind of peace and excitement that came from emptying his balls into her beautiful mouth, yes, but it went deeper than that too. He was enjoying himself around her. Dominating her, looking after her, making her laugh and tremble and squirm and obey. It felt good. It felt real.

Which, of course, it wasn't. Or, at least, their marriage wasn't real. And he had to keep reminding himself of that. This was a short-term thing. Peach was most likely only doing this for his wallet. She was enjoying herself too — that was clear — but he doubted whether she'd be enjoying herself half as much if it wasn't for the ten million dollars. And who could blame her? She was sensible to take what he was offering her.

There was this tiny part of Isaac, though, that worried that this wouldn't be happening if it wasn't for his money. A girl like Peach, so young and generously-proportioned and bouncy and full of life, would never be interested in a grump like him. Aging, hardened by life and all its disappointments, unable to have fun.

Still. What did it matter? If Peach was having a good time right now, and he could afford all the nice things he was buying her, where was the harm? He'd regret it if he didn't at least allow his cock a good time.

"Your bathroom is soooo nice," said Peach, bringing him out of his reverie.

He dipped a sponge in the water and began running it slowly down her back.

"Mmmm, that feels good." He heard the quiet clink of her butt plug on the bottom of the bath as she shifted positions, then he saw her pulling a yellow rubber duck out of the water. "It's funny to think about you having rubber duckies, Daddy," she said, giggling. "Do you use them every time you have a bath?"

"They're for guests," Isaac said moodily.

Peach was silent for a moment. Isaac noticed her spine had stiffened. "Do you have a lot of those, then? Guests, I mean?"

Isaac took a long deep breath, then exhaled slowly. "Nope. None at all, really."

"None?" Peach said, taken aback. "But you have such a big home. And you never share it with anyone?"

"I've been busy lately," Isaac replied. "Well, I've been busy all my life, really." He noticed how sad he felt when he said this. Had his entire life been in vain? All this hard work, and for what?

"I guess that's how you got so rich," Peach said. "Although I feel like I worked hard all my life, and somehow I ended up poor as dirt."

"Wealth is one part hard work and one part luck," Isaac told her. "Plus, you've got to be pretty bloody-minded too. Willing to sacrifice anything and anyone that gets in your way."

Peach looked at him, screwing up her nose. "But... why? Doesn't that make you feel kinda yucky?"

Isaac laughed. "Yes, sweetheart. It does make me feel kinda yucky. But I did it all for a reason. Originally, at least. I did it because I wanted to try to buy back my family ranch."

"Your family ranch?" asked Peach. "Is this the one you told me about? The reason we're getting married?"

Isaac felt a pang of grief. "Yes," he said. "It should have been mine. My father always told me it would be mine after he died. But nobody could find the paperwork after he... after my parents both..." In spite of himself, he noticed tears collecting in his eyes. But immediately, the tears were replaced by the bitter taste of anger on his tongue. "My aunt got it. She had an older will. From before I was born. The whole place went to her. And she says she'll never sell it to me. Not unless—"

"Unless you're married?" Peach cut in quietly. "But... why?"

"Because she's old-fashioned and stuck in her ways, partly. But also because she's downright mean. She knows I'm not the marrying type. She thinks I'm a player. Thinks I'll never settle down with just one woman... And more to the point, I think she thinks no woman would ever want to marry me."

Peach opened her mouth, like she wanted to say something, but then she closed it again. She fidgeted, her glass plug clinking softly on the bottom of the tub again.

"Daddy," said Peach shyly. "Would you like to get in here with me?"

Isaac smiled at her. The thought of joining this smooth goddess in the water was almost unbearably good. But he had to hold back. "No," he said firmly. "I can't."

Peach looked hurt. "You wouldn't like to get naked with me?"

Isaac ran the sponge across her back. "It's not a good idea. I don't know how close I could be to you naked without..."

Peach ran her tongue across her lips. Damn, she was beautiful. "And would it be so bad if we...?"

Isaac felt his cock thickening, begging him to just get in the goddamn bath with her. "We can't," Isaac snapped. "We can't fuck or we won't be able to get the marriage annulled. It's the quickest way to reverse the marriage. If we engage in intercourse this close to the wedding, we're in serious trouble. For one thing, it's likely to happen again. Especially if it feels as good as I think it would feel." He took a breath. "And for another, it's so close to the wedding that a lawyer might argue that we basically consummated it anyway. Then we're looking at a lengthy divorce process. A ton of paperwork. Unnecessary costs."

Peach pouted. She shifted yet again, and he heard the telltale clink, then noticed the tiny flutter of her eyelashes as the pleasure no doubt coursed through her. "Oh," she said. "Well, I don't want to make things hard for you."

Oh, you're making them hard, babygirl.

"Hmm," Isaac said, running the sponge down her back, a little lower this time, brushing the cleft between her ass cheeks, "I guess there are other ways I could penetrate you." He swallowed. "Ways that don't *legally* count as sexual intercourse."

Suddenly, Peach's eyes shone with hope.

"Get out of the bath, babygirl," Isaac said, his voice deep and certain.

Peach did as she was told, holding onto the edge of the rolltop bath, lifting her gorgeous, full body out of it, and stepping onto his bathmat, dripping wet.

He could hardly believe how privileged he was, getting to be the man standing there looking at her right now. Those breasts, man. He could lose himself for days between them. Just place his head between them, kissing and licking and grabbing great big generous handfuls of her, the luckiest man in the world to be able to touch such a perfectly womanly woman.

But right now, this wasn't a time for kissing and licking.

"I'm going to enter you," Isaac began.

Dutifully, Peach got down onto her knees, opening her mouth wide for him.

But he stopped her. "I'm not going to fuck your mouth this time, babygirl."

She looked up at him, confusion distorting her features. He reached down to her mouth, gently closing her jaw, then pushing his finger between her lips, just for a moment, to feel the warmth of her. She sucked him happily, as though he was a pacifier, and every trace of worry disappeared from her face. Slowly, as she sucked, she began rubbing her ass on the bathroom tiles, enjoying the sensation of the plug she'd been wearing for over an hour.

He knew she'd be ready by now.

"Stand up," he instructed her, "and grab onto the sink."

She did so, and he looked in wonder at the plug, still wedged perfectly between her cheeks. That cute little teddy bear still looked happy as ever to be there.

"Babygirl," he said, "I'm gonna take your plug out in just a moment. And now that you're nice and stretched from it, I'm going to put my cock in you."

"Yes, Daddy," said Peach, looking up at the reflection in the mirror over the sink.

Isaac could scarcely believe how beautiful she looked. Those pouty lips. Those sparkling blue eyes. That messy blond hair, curling in soft ringlets from the steam in the bath.

Then, he looked back down at her buttocks. So warm and inviting. He grabbed hold of his rock-hard cock and guided it firmly between her ass cheeks. The bubbly, oily bathwater acted as the perfect lubricant, and within moments, he was squeezing his dick into her tight, hot hole. It was heaven.

"You're a good girl, Peach Trimble," said Isaac, his voice strained as he slid deep into her private passage. "Daddy's very pleased with you indeed."

"Thank you, sir," said Peach softly. "It makes me happy to please you."

He noticed that her voice was strained too. Catching as she spoke. Breathless from the pleasure he was giving her.

He began to slide in and out, gently at first, as he got the measure of how much she could take. "That okay for you?" he asked, brushing her hair away from her face, so he could see her expressions clearly in the mirror.

"Mm-hmm," she whispered. "You can do it harder if you want, Daddy."

His cock swelled with excitement inside of her. "Alright, babygirl," he said. "Hold on tight."

He began thrusting in and out of her ass now, rough and hard and unrestrained, grabbing onto her hips so hard his fingers left marks on her. He fucked her as though it was the first time in his life he was truly learning how to live. He fucked her as though he finally meant it. He fucked her as though everything between them was real. And then, when he came, it felt like he'd never stop.

Chapter Twelve

PEACH

NORMALLY, PEACH WAS A light sleeper. She supposed that had something to do with living alone in a rough part of town. Always keeping one eye open in case of danger. A squeak at the door. A creak of the floorboard. A scream of a siren. A yell of a drunk. There were so many noises in a bad neighborhood of a less-than-ideal city that even if you did feel safe enough to sleep, the racket would wake you up anyway.

Not so on Star Island. On Star Island, you heard nothing but soft ocean waves, crickets, and your own breath.

And the breath of the man next to you, in Peach's case.

It was only her second night on the island, but already, Peach was sleeping in a brand-new mansion. Isaac's place.

How had things moved so fast? Peach had lain there, in his enormous Alaskan King Size bed, which, according to Isaac, was the biggest-sized bed out there. She had tried to think back, looking for clues as to the moment that their deal had switched over from pure business to something more. Had his intentions been to dominate her sexually all along? Unlikely, given the fact he'd been at such pains to explain the fake marriage plan. What about the moment she first entered his home? Unlikely, given how scruffy she'd looked after running from the airport.

Whenever it had happened, something definitely *had* switched. He'd come three times yesterday. Once on her ass while spanking her, once down her throat, which was also full of ice-cream, and once inside her pre-stretched bottom. And, crazy and unexpected as it all had been, she'd loved every damn minute of it.

What he hadn't done yet was made *her* come. She got the feeling that was part of her punishment yesterday. Teasing her, making her be a good girl for him, making her want to come so fricking badly that she could have stayed up all night having orgasm after orgasm if he'd let her.

The thing was, though, he *didn't* let her. After emptying his load deep inside her, he'd given her a pair of his silky pajamas — which fit her perfectly because of her plus-size body — and he'd made her warm milk and cookies, and he'd tucked her up in his bed and read her fairytales until she fell asleep.

Cinderella.

Beauty and the Beast.

Little Red Riding Wolf.

She'd seen something of her own situation in all of them. But instead of reading into them too deeply, or getting herself all worked up about the Prince Charming Beast-Wolf who also happened to be her fiancé, she had fallen into a deep, relaxing sleep, and she hadn't stirred once until morning.

When she woke up, she realized that she had traveled all the way across the huge expanse of mattress, and she had somehow curled up her body into the Little Spoon, her but pressed up against his morning glory.

"Morning beautiful," Isaac whispered in his ear. "You know, you're very cute when you're asleep."

"I am?" Peach asked, feeling vulnerable. "Did I snore?"

"Nope," Isaac replied. "You sucked your thumb and mumbled babytalk at me. It was adorable."

"If you say so," Peach said, cheeks burning. She started turning to face him, but Isaac's hand grabbed her wrist in a flash, holding her where she was.

"Keep that bottom where it is for a minute," he said, pressing his hardness between her cheeks. He was in boxers, she was in silk pajamas, but that didn't stop the two of them doing everything they could to get that butt-fuck going in spite of their clothes.

"Want me to take my jammies off, Daddy?" Peach asked, pressing her bottom cheeks down onto the engorged tip of his cock, as far as they would go before her PJs got in the way.

Isaac growled. "You know I do, babygirl. But I'm not gonna take you in the ass this morning."

"You're not?" Peach asked, still rubbing her ass up and down on his rock-hard appendage.

"You better stop that right now, Little one," Isaac said. "Or you'll make Daddy mess up his boxers." He grabbed hold of her pajama bottoms, whipping them down in one swift movement. Then, he flipped Peach over onto her back.

She squealed, feeling suddenly vulnerable, her legs bare and wide, her pussy fully on display to him for the first time. But she only had to look at the mountain in Isaac's boxers to know that he was happy with what he saw.

"Daddy's very proud of you for waiting so patiently for this," he told her. "It's important that you know that Daddy's in charge of your pleasure. Every orgasm you receive is down to Daddy now. You will come when Daddy wants you to, and you will make Daddy come when he wants it too."

Peach bit her lip. "And what does Daddy want now?"

Isaac looked into her eyes. "Daddy wants you to come all over his mouth, babygirl. And when Daddy's done, he's going to spray your tits with his cum, and you're going to lie in his bed, full of his hot cum, while he makes you breakfast in bed."

Peach wriggled on the mattress. "O-o-kay," she said, trying to sound cool. But already her pussy was wet and aching for him.

"What you mean to say is 'Yes, Daddy.'"

"Yes, Daddy," said Peach. "Yes to all of it, sir."

Isaac grabbed hold of her thighs, yanking them farther apart, and then he pushed his face down between her legs, breathing her in.

Peach felt momentarily embarrassed. She'd had a bath last night, but she didn't know how much of — herself — she smelled of right now. She needn't have worried, though, because almost immediately Isaac was making a noise that showed that he was very pleased with what he'd found down there.

"I could worship this pussy for days, babygirl," he said, dipping his face down low and running his tongue up her slit until the tip reached her clit. She felt her lips quivering under his touch, slackening and opening for him a little, willing him to enter her. But he didn't. His tongue stayed fixed on her clit, licking and sucking and working it as she dripped with pleasure for him.

His hands pinned her down, grabbing fistfuls of her soft flesh, holding her down like she was the last woman on earth and he never wanted to let her go.

"I think you're going to make me..." she panted.

Already, she was soaking the Alaskan King mattress. The white sheets of Alaska, snowy and pure. The red-hot fire in her pussy, melting the ice with her arousal. Fire and ice. Cum and ice-cream. Him and her.

She was full of their contradictions, full of desire for this man who was her opposite, full of shuddering lust for his velvet-smooth mouth and satin-smooth dick. She arched her back with the impossibleness of feeling inside her, as though she was trying to escape it, and then suddenly… it escaped her. She cried out as her body tensed and released, as her moisture dribbled down his mouth and his newly-stubbled chin, as her body gave him what he had asked of her.

He drank her down like hot melted ice-cream.

And when he was done, he kneeled before her, his cock thick and upright as a monument. A monument to their desire for one another. He took one of her small hands in his, and he wrapped it around his girth, with his hand on top of hers, showing her just how fast he liked it, how hard he liked it, how much of it was needed.

And then, at the very same moment that a small moan escaped his lip, a hot jet of cum sprayed across her belly, her nipples, her throat, and he painted her with his pleasure.

He looked down at her, smiling. He dipped his finger in his cum, then spread it across her breast a little farther. "Good," he said. "It suits you."

Peach blushed, slightly embarrassed. She'd never have guessed that someone as restrained and nerdy-looking as Isaac would have been so filthy in the bedroom. But then most men wouldn't have known that she'd be so dirty and happy to surrender to his perverse fantasies either. Maybe they'd met their match.

"How'd you like your eggs?" Isaac asked her.

She looked down at her body, lined with glistening cum. "Runny," she said with a giggle.

*

"The eggs were good, Daddy," Peach said, pushing aside the fancy foldable table that Isaac had brought to the bed. "Even if I *do* have your naughty juice drying all over my skin."

Isaac had finished his breakfast long before her, and seemed to have been enjoying watching her eat. "Daddy could watch you eat breakfast covered in his cum every day," he said.

"If you bring me scrambled eggs and blueberry muffins in bed every day then it's a deal," Peach said.

Out of nowhere, Isaac slapped her on the thigh, up near the ass. It wasn't a hard slap, though. It was a playful one. It sent ripples of excitement through her.

"What's next, Daddy?" she asked. "Are we going to take a shower together?"

"No," said Isaac. "That would take us far too long, and we have things to do. Places to be."

"We do?"

"We do."

Peach wrinkled her nose. "Don't you have work today, Daddy?"

"Yes, but I have two hours until my first meeting. And the office won't fall apart without me. So, I figured we could use that time wisely."

"Like how?"

"Well, I believe I owe you a new stuffie," said Isaac. "And then... well. How about I keep that as a surprise? You'll find out soon enough."

Peach clapped her hands together in excitement. "Can we bring Teddy?"

Teddy had stayed with the dog-sitter last night. Isaac had arranged it without prompting, surprising Peach with his thoughtfulness.

"You know what?" Isaac said, stroking her forearm. "Why not? Let's take Teddy."

Peach almost fainted with shock. "For real?"

Isaac looked suddenly serious. "For real."

*

"I'd forgotten you said you were going to buy me a stuffie!" Peach said, carrying her brand new cuddly bear in her arms. "But you know, you really didn't need to buy me the biggest one in the store!"

The bear was big and white and completely impractical for walking through a busy shopping mall. But the reason Peach had chosen it is because it had looked *very* similar to the one she had worn on the butt plug last night. And the thought of that made her feel naughty in a good way.

"You bet I needed to buy you the biggest one in the store," Isaac replied. "What kind of Daddy am I if I don't spoil my Little girl rotten?"

Peach was going to make a playful comment about the fact that she was having to carry the massive bear all by herself, but the fact was, she'd insisted on it. Plus, Isaac was carrying all the other shopping bags, as well as walking Teddy. It was amazing to see him holding the leash, walking Teddy as if he was his owner. He looked so comfortable with the dog, it was hard to believe he was actually an animal-hater. The only problem was that ever since they'd taken the dog out with them, Isaac's eyes had been pink and watery, and he kept sneezing.

"You sure you're okay walking Teddy, Daddy? I mean, with your allergies?"

"It's not so bad so long as we stay outside with him," Isaac replied.

It felt like progress to hear Isaac referring to Teddy as "him" and not "it" anymore.

They were at Bal Harbor, an upscale *al fresco* mall. There was an array of luxury designer boutiques, as well as large open courtyards with palm trees, tropical flowers, and limestone fountains. There was Chanel. Gucci. Prada. And of course, the fanciest toy store she'd ever set foot in. It made Build-A-Bear look like the most basic place in the world. Not that her new bear was going to be any more loved than her build-A-Bear stuffie of Chase. Peach had room in her heart for endless stuffies. But it was true that the bear she'd been given just now was always going to be extremely special.

"You thought of a name for that bear yet?" Isaac asked as they maneuvered around a pond full of exotic koi carp.

Peach thought for a moment. "Hey, how about Alaska? He's big, but not too big for our Alaskan-sized bed!" The moment she said that, her tummy lurched.

Our bed.

Isaac's bed didn't belong to her. They weren't an "us" or a "we". She didn't want to sound presumptuous or greedy. He was letting her stay in a mansion of her very own. With a bed of her very own. Last night was just a bit of fun. Okay, a *lot* of fun. But that was all.

"You know what?" Isaac replied. "I think you're right. But there's only one way to know for sure."

Peach stopped walking and turned to him. "There is?"

"We'd better take him home and put it to the test."

Peach felt herself growing dizzy with lust. Was Isaac suggesting what she thought he was suggesting? Another long session between his sheets? Another night pretending that they were about to become Mr. And Mrs. Righton for real?

She looked into Isaac's eyes. Dark and serious behind those black-framed glasses. She looked at his chin, sprouting with stubble because he'd spent the morning giving her pleasure instead of giving *himself* a shave. His muscular physique. She'd seen his cock. She'd tasted it. She'd watched it squirt cum all over her. But she hadn't even seen his torso yet. His abs. His pecs.

I want you, Isaac Righton. I want you bad.

"Babygirl?" he said, looking amused.

"Yes, Daddy?"

"You're drooling, darling."

"Oh!" Peach wiped her chin, embarrassed, but Isaac didn't seem bothered by her faux-pas. In fact, he seemed to like it when she was a little foolish. "So, are we going back now then?" she asked, trying to distract him from the fact she'd literally just slobbered while thinking about his big Daddy-dong. "Or are we going to do a bit more shopping? Maybe check out Gucci or Prada? Or one of those other stores with an Italian name I can't pronounce?"

Isaac smiled. "I think we've shopped 'til we've dropped."

It was true. Isaac had been so generous. He'd bought Peach eight new pairs of Agent Provocateur panties costing over a hundred dollars a pair. There was a pair with pink ribbons down the front, which actually opened if you pulled them, making them into crotchless panties. There was a lilac pair with a pink cherry on. A black pair with DADDY'S GIRL written on it in crystals, which of course he had to get for her. There was also a pair he bought without her looking from the bridal section, and she was so impatient to find out what he'd got she could have exploded.

Plus, he'd bought her some other naughty lingerie. Bodysuits and corsets and playsuits that were basically just collars with chains attached. All of these things, he said, would show off her curves.

He'd bought her some cute pink sequin sneakers from designer footwear store Addict too, plus a t-shirt with strawberries all over it from Monnalisa, a store meant for kids, but she saw the top in the window and fell in love with it so Isaac got it for her. He told her he didn't mind if she spilled out of it a little bit. In fact, he said, he'd like that.

"You're right, Daddy," she said. "We'll go back then."

"Not yet," Isaac told her firmly. "There's something we gotta do first."

Something about that tone made Peach freeze. "There is?"

"Mm-hmm," he said, looking her in the eye. "Brunch."

Peach sighed with relief. "Oh, right! Brunch! But... you made me breakfast this morning. Isn't it a little early?"

"I'm building up quite the appetite when I'm around you," said Isaac. "Besides, this place does the best buttermilk pancakes."

Peach rubbed her tummy in anticipation. "It's a date."

"Good," he said. "But before you go in, I want you to go change into your first pair of panties. The purple ones with the cherry. I want your pussy to be thinking about me while you eat."

Peach wanted to say: *My pussy's always thinking about you, Daddy.* But she didn't, because she was a good girl.

Chapter Thirteen

ISAAC

I SAAC FELT NERVOUS AS they headed for the French brasserie. Not because he thought she wouldn't like the restaurant. He knew she'd be into it. A fun and funky France-meets-Florida eatery, with *fruits de mer* to die for.

No. The thing he hadn't told her yet, the whole reason they were here, in fact, was because he'd arranged a surprise for her. The kind of surprise that she was going to hate at first. But hopefully, over the next half hour or so, the kind of surprise that would mean the world to her.

Isaac had invited her friends to lunch: Daisy and Kiera. They were the reason that Peach had been crying when he'd seen her in Dade-D Bar, the day he'd suggested they fake-marry one another. But the reason Peach had been crying was because she felt like her friends didn't care about her anymore, and Isaac knew that was impossible. You didn't meet a girl like Peach Trimble and go off her. In fact, the girl had a way of growing on you like an erection.

"I don't even know what a brasserie is," said Peach nervously, having returned from the public bathroom, where she'd changed into her cherry panties just as he'd asked. She told him the soft fabric tickled her pussy lips a bit, which was perfect. He wanted her to remember that her pussy belonged to him from now on.

"There's something you should know before we get there," he told her.

"Let me guess," she replied. "We're gonna have to leave Teddy outside?"

Hearing his name, Teddy looked up at Peach and whined.

"It's okay, boy," said Isaac to the dog. "You can stay with us. I got us a table outside. But you're gonna have to sit on the other side of the table to me."

He had to admit, the dog was cute. It made his eyes itch like hell but it had a ton of attitude, especially with that little topknot Peach had given him. He was starting to view the dog as an extension of Peach. You didn't get one without the other. Teddy was part of Peach. And if he wanted to be close to her, he had to be close to the canine too. It was worth having his eyes itch like hell.

Unfortunately, Teddy couldn't come into his house until he'd gotten rid of the cat. He'd probably smell the thing in an instant and start chasing it all over the house. Yesterday, he'd had to keep it shut downstairs so that Peach didn't find it. He just didn't want her getting the wrong impression about him. Thinking he was some kind of pet-loving Papa. He was worried, frankly, that she'd fall for him under false pretenses.

But... was she falling for him anyway?

And, more to the point... was he falling for her?

No. Surely not. It was way too soon for that. It was just lust. Nothing less, nothing more. And as soon as he'd married her, and as soon as they'd got the marriage annulled, they'd probably test out their feelings with a proper fuck, and they'd realize that was all it had been: a desire to have the un-have-able.

"Is that what you were going to tell me?" Peach asked impatiently. "That you got us a table outside?"

Isaac stopped staring at the dog and looked back at Peach. "No. It was something else. I wanted to tell you that we're going to have company."

"Company?" Peach looked over at the restaurant nervously. "Is it your Daddy friends?"

"No, actually," Isaac replied. "It's your Little friends."

Peach took a step back. "Oh. No. That's very kind of you but I can't..."

"Sweetheart," Isaac told her. "We're getting married tomorrow. They're your best friends. I'd never forgive myself if we didn't at least invite them."

"The invitations are ready?" Peach asked.

"They're in my bag."

"But what if they... what if they say no? What if they try to stop me? What if they don't believe that we...?"

Isaac gripped her shoulder and gave it a squeeze. "That's a lot of what ifs, babygirl. Let's go find out, shall we? And then we'll take it from there?"

Peach looked up at him, and it almost broke his heart to see how much trust there was in her eyes. Not because she wasn't right to trust him — it just felt like such an honor. To have someone so pure and sweet relying on him so completely. He couldn't let her down.

"Come on," he said. "Let's go fill our bellies with pancakes. And invite your best buddies to the greatest wedding in town."

"I don't know..." said Peach, walking quietly behind him, hiding behind her bear as they approached the restaurant.

*

Daisy and Kiera had both turned up, which was something. Daisy looked right at home in a place like this. Since she'd gotten engaged to Montague, she'd started wearing expensive clothes from a specialist Little boutique partnered up with Daddies Inc. She wore a dress covered in smiling sunflowers today, though she wasn't smiling herself.

Kiera, a redhead with red freckles and more of a punky look, seemed slightly out of place. The piercings. The blue hair. The green lipstick. It was like she'd teleported here from the 1980s and didn't quite know what to make of it.

"What's going on, Daisy?" asked Kiera. "Why are we here? And why's the dog-phobic dude the one who invited us?"

Peach cast Isaac an apologetic glance, then looked back at her friends. "It's so good to see you both," she said, an anxious wobble evident in her voice. "Thank you for coming."

"I don't get it," said Daisy. "I thought you were back in Connecticut. We said goodbye at the airport. Did you come back already? Does this have something to do with that text you sent me, asking for Isaac's number?" Daisy looked at Isaac now. "Isaac. Is Peach in some kind of trouble?"

Isaac didn't know Daisy too well, in spite of the fact she was engaged to his best friend and worked in his office. Montague liked to keep Daisy to himself outside of work, which was fair enough given how busy they all were. When Montague managed to get time off, he wanted to spend it with his girl. Isaac got that. But it meant that he only really knew Daisy in a business capacity. And since she was Montague's PA, not his, he didn't even know her that well in a business capacity either.

"Everything's okay, Daisy," he told her. "Trust me."

Daisy looked wary. "I'm assuming she sent you an angry message after I gave her your number. She was mad at you for telling her to take Teddy out of the Daddies Inc offices. But—"

"It's not that," Isaac told her. As he spoke to Daisy, he could feel Kiera giving him daggers. She was a tough cookie, that one. He had to get this right for Peach's sake. "Peach and I didn't get off to the best start," he said. "It's true. But... things have developed between us since then. We've both been having a lot of strong feelings. Feelings that have been difficult to ignore."

He looked at Peach, sitting there in that little dress. He pictured the cherry panties on her perfect little pussy. The pussy he'd sucked and tasted this morning, the pussy that had climaxed on the tip of his tongue.

"We're getting married," he said, cutting to the chase.

Daisy's face turned instantly pale. "You're *what*?"

"To *you*?" Kiera asked rudely. Clearly, she wasn't his biggest fan.

"Yes," Peach said, cutting in. "I'm marrying Isaac. He's a good man, and we... we... we..."

"We have feelings for one another," Isaac said, helping her out.

"Yes," Peach said, smiling gratefully. "We have feelings for one another."

The pancakes arrived at the table and everyone remained silent, but the moment they had gone, Daisy said: "Why didn't you tell me something was going on between you? Why didn't you tell me you never made it back to Connecticut? Why am I only hearing about this now?" Her eyes filled with tears. "I thought we were best friends."

Kiera huffed. "She thinks she's too good for us now. With her massive designer teddy bear."

Alaska the bear was so big that the restaurant had given him a seat of his very own, next to Peach. It had seemed fun to Isaac, like something they could have all laughed about. It wasn't fair of Kiera to make fun of the bear like that. Just ten minutes ago, Alaska had made Peach so happy.

Suddenly, Daisy leaned forward. "Wait," she said. "Did Montague know about this?"

"I asked him not to tell you for a day or two," Isaac told her. "It's my fault. Things were just moving so fast, and I wanted to be sure—"

"You asked my Daddy to lie to me?"

"Told you he was bad news," Kiera said with a snort.

Fuck. This wasn't going well at all. Isaac squeezed Peach's hand under the table to give her support. She didn't squeeze back.

"I know this is a lot to take in," Isaac said. "But Peach and I would really like you to be there. At the wedding. And I'm sure when you see how happy we are—"

"You're talking about the wedding like it's about to happen already," Daisy said, raising an eyebrow. "When is it happening? In a week? In a month? In a year?"

Isaac reached into his pocket, pulling out two pristine invitations. Hopefully, these would show Daisy and Kiera what a good guy Isaac was. He'd had them made with a gold leaf border, and in the center, there was a cartoon depiction of Peach and himself. They had both been drawn to look like members of PAW Patrol. He was Chase, in a police uniform. She was Skye, in a pink pilot's outfit. It was the first time Peach had seen the invitations too, and he heard the breath catch in her throat.

"What the heck?" said Daisy, picking up one of the invitations and glaring at it. She didn't seem interested in the cartoon dog versions of him and Peach. She was staring at the words. "You're getting married *tomorrow?* At Dade-D Bar?"

Peach took a look at the invitation, her lower lip trembling. "Er, yes. Apparently so."

Daisy stood up, her chair screeching on the polished floor as she did so. "Come on, Kiera. We're leaving."

"But... but... pancakes..." Peach said.

"Eff the pancakes!" Daisy hissed, tears streaming down her cheeks. Isaac knew that her Daddy would have been very angry to hear her cussing like that, but at least she'd said it quiet enough that nobody else could hear.

After that, Daisy stormed off.

Kiera watched her go, then stood up too. "If you wanted to punish us for moving to Miami, you could have done it in a less mean way," Kiera said, frowning. "You just ruined Daisy's wedding. Some friend you are."

Kiera left too, and Peach turned to Isaac, unable to hold back the tears.

"Oh, darling," Isaac said. "I'm so sorry. I was trying to do something nice. I messed up."

Tears fell heavily on Peach's cheeks, and then, finally, she stopped crying. She shuddered a few times as the tears died down, then her expression became blank and unreadable.

There was a long, terrible moment of silence between them. Isaac imagined the many ways that Peach might have been about to break off their wedding.

"I hate having to lie to my friends," she said, whimpering. "That's why I couldn't see them before the wedding."

"But sweetheart," Isaac said, stroking her face, wiping away her tears with his thumb. "That's the thing. I didn't say one word of a lie to them."

Peach looked away, as if trying to remember all the things that they'd said. Eventually, she turned to him. "Nor did I, Daddy." She looked down at the invitation, running her finger over the gold leaf. "This is really beautiful, you know."

"Like you," Isaac replied. It was corny, but he didn't care. This wonderful girl of his made him feel feelings he thought he'd never get the chance to feel.

"I still want to marry you," Peach said softly.

"I still want to marry you," Isaac replied.

"And I still want to eat all my pancakes," Peach said with a small giggle.

"That's my girl," Isaac replied. He pushed Daisy's plate a little closer to hers. "And you know what? It looks like today's brunch just turned into an All You Can Eat buffet. So don't stop until your belly aches."

Peach laughed a big laugh now. "Okay, Daddy. Anyone would think you're trying to fatten me up for this wedding."

"All I want is for you to stay exactly as you are, Peach Trimble," Isaac replied. And he meant it.

Just then, a man in an orange jacket walked up to them. He was in his fifties, with a long, gray ponytail and a scruffy beard.

"Sorry to interrupt your meal," he said, "but have you heard about the Defenders of Wildlife charity? I'm collecting donations for them today."

Isaac felt his blood start to boil. He was in the middle of a moment. Having brunch. There was a time and a place to ask for handouts and this wasn't one of them.

"Not interested," he grunted, with a dismissive wave of the hand. "Leave us alone."

The man walked away, and when Isaac turned around to look at Peach, she was open-mouthed with shock. "The Defenders of Wildlife are amazing," she said. "They help sea turtles and polar bears and manatees. We should have listened to the guy."

Isaac smiled at her. "I'd rather listen to you telling me which pancake topping you prefer: this one, that one, or all of them."

Peach smiled, but he knew that he had messed up a bit. He'd be sure to make it up to her later.

Chapter Fourteen

PEACH

PEACH LOOKED DOWN AT her panties as she peed. They were so exquisite. The most expensive thing to have ever touched her private parts, that was for sure.

She was peeing like a racehorse. Back at the restaurant, she'd drunk so much juice, and eaten so many pancakes, that she could have spent the rest of the day lying on the couch groaning, rubbing her belly, and watching cartoons. But Isaac had other ideas.

He wasn't at home right now. He'd had to go to work after the restaurant, which had sucked given how crappy the meeting with her friends had gone. Plus there had been that weird thing with the Defenders of Wildlife guy. Sure, he'd interrupted their breakfast to ask them for money and that didn't seem quite right. But at the end of the day, the endangered species of this world needed urgent help and Isaac could have been more considerate.

Still, it wasn't like he wasn't considerate with *her*. He'd arranged for his driver to pick her up, and she'd enjoyed looking at all her new things back at the house. She was wearing her new sparkly sneakers indoors, which was fine because they were brand new and clean. And she had put on her strawberry t-shirt, which was definitely too tight, especially after all those pancakes, but it was super cute so what did it matter?

Then, of course, there was Alaska. The biggest teddy bear in human history. She'd have to wait until tonight to see if he fit in Isaac's bed. That is, if he let her sleep with him. Everything felt so unknown right now. She was getting married tomorrow. Did that mean she had to spend the night alone? She wasn't sure if it was bad luck to spend the night with her husband-to-be if it was only ever going to be a fake wedding.

But... was it fake?

Isaac had pretty much admitted to her at the restaurant that he had feelings for her. But as for what those feelings were, she wasn't exactly sure. She knew what *her* feelings were. They were backflips in her tummy. They were fireworks in her brain and sparkles in her secret place.

It was confusing, though, because at a time like this, she would have liked nothing more than to celebrate with Kiera and Daisy. They'd be so happy for her if they understood how good she felt when she was with him. And they'd be so very, very angry if they knew that the marriage was a fake.

Oh, it was all so complicated. But right now, Daddy had given Peach some orders. "Go home," he'd told her, "and spend some time in Little Space. You have another hour of free time on your schedule before anyone is due to visit you, and I want you to use it wisely."

"Is watching cartoons in my underwear using my time wisely, Daddy?" she'd asked him, fluttering her lashes.

"Nope," he'd replied. "Cartoons are for good girls who've had a balanced and active day. I want you to do one of the following activities: coloring in, coming up with a new dance routine, or having a stuffie tea party."

Peach had known instantly which of those appealed to her. "I can introduce Chase and Alaska!" she had said, clapping her hands together.

When Isaac had said goodbye to her, he'd given her a small kiss on the lips. It struck her that it was the first time that they'd kissed, and it felt magic. His warmth, his realness, up close and personal with her in public. It didn't feel like they were putting on a show, like they were nothing but business partners concocting a sneaky plan. It felt like he had wanted to kiss her. It felt like he had wanted to push his body up against hers and... claim her.

She shivered with lust, trying not to think naughty thoughts as she finally finished peeing. Wearing these panties, being alone in the house... it was enough to put ideas in her head... But Daddy had told her she wasn't allowed to touch herself without his permission. Daddy had told her to spend some time in Little Space. So that was what she was going to do.

She came out of the bathroom and lifted Alaska up off the couch. "Come here, big boy," she told him. She placed him on one of the tall stools at the kitchen counter. Being even wider than a human being, he wobbled a little to begin with. "Sit nicely for the tea party," she told him. "I have a very special guest to introduce to you."

Alaska smiled happily at her and she couldn't help thinking about the butt plug that had stretched her wide in preparation for Daddy's cock last night.

"Ooof," she said. "It's going to be hard not to think naughty thoughts with you around, Alaska, my boy."

She took the elevator upstairs to her bedroom, trying to find Chase. The room was a mess. She'd only spent one night there so far, but she'd chucked her clothes and toys around so chaotically it looked like a bomb had gone off.

"Oops," she said to herself. "Daddy wouldn't like this."

Before she'd set foot here, Isaac's place had been completely pristine. She guessed that was probably quite easy when you had as many people working for you as he did. Plus, it seemed like before she came along, he basically lived in the office. Even so, she couldn't imagine him doing anything as wild as throwing his clothes across the room! He wasn't that sort of guy. And before she'd met him, she'd have probably mocked a guy like that. Called him boring or a Serious Sam.

But being around him was rubbing off on her. She wanted to be a person who had nice things. There was no shame in that. Everybody wanted nice things, didn't they? And if she had nice things, she was going to have to treat them nicely.

Before she knew what she was doing, she was folding up pants and hanging up shirts in the closet. She was arranging toys on her dresser and even humming to herself happily as she did it. All the while, Teddy looked up at her with his head cocked to one side.

What is my human doing? he seemed to be asking. *Why is my human doing this tidying thing? She's never done it before! Should I be concerned?*

In spite of Teddy's judgy face, it was satisfying work. It even made her full tummy feel better to be moving around like this.

By the time she was done, Chase was looking impatient with her.

"I want a tea party! Ruff!" he barked at her.

"Sorry, Chasey," she said. "Let's go downstairs and meet Alaska."

She walked downstairs, deciding that Daddy would prefer her to be active instead of taking the elevator again. But she let Chase slide down the banister because she was trying to get back into Little Space after all that sensible tidying up she'd just done.

Alaska was right where she'd left him, like a good bear, and she placed Chase down on the countertop opposite him.

"You two have absolutely nothing in common," she told them, "but I think you're going to get on swimmingly."

She grabbed two of the smallest mugs from the cupboard and placed them down in front of the stuffies.

"Oh, I almost forgot," she said. "Alaska, you should probably know that Chase smells of bubblegum. And he makes this noise."

Peach squished Chase's tummy and the PAW Patrol theme tune played out of the muffled speaker inside him.

Immediately, Teddy began yelping with that finger-nails-down-a-chalkboard bark of his. Then, he began running around, chasing an invisible intruder, growling at pairs of shoes, ornaments, and even the coffee table as the song played.

Peach couldn't stop laughing. "Teddy, you silly-billy! It's just a song playing in Chase's tummy! But it's good to know you're such an amazing guard dog!"

Teddy looked up at her and she lifted up the Chase toy. "Look!" She squished the tummy again, trying to show Teddy where the noise had come from. The second the song started up again, Teddy began his crazy act, running around the house even faster this time, knocking over an expensive-looking Greek-style vase.

Time seemed to slow down to a standstill as the vase tumbled down. Peach reached her hands out toward it, but there was no chance of getting there in time.

"No!" screamed Peach as the vase shattered to pieces. Just as she began picking up, she heard a deep voice above her.

"Ms. Trimble," it said. "It's time to get your life in order."

*

Peach was sitting on the couch with a cup of coffee in one hand and a questionnaire in the other.

Opposite her was Dan, her life coach. They'd spent a little time together the other day, but hadn't done much because she'd been so busy and tired. Today though, it seemed like Dan had plenty of things for them to do. Dan was dressed more like a sports coach than a life coach, and he had a whistle around his neck.

"Well?" Dan asked. "Have you had a chance to answer all the questions?"

"I... I don't think I can answer any of them," Peach said unsurely.

Dan tapped his fingers on the arm of the couch with an air of impatience. Peach wondered why Isaac had even booked a life coach for her. Was it because he'd seen her crying in Dade-D Bar? Was it because he thought her life was a mess?

Dan took the questionnaire off her. "Let's go through some of the easier ones. Here." He pointed at one of the early questions. "What would you say is your primary objective in life?"

"Um. To have a good time?"

Dan chuckled. "Well, sure. But what drives you? A desire for wealth? A desire to help others?"

"Both, I guess?" said Peach uncertainly.

"Alright," said Dan. "Let's examine that. You're about to receive a large sum of money. Do you want to use the majority of it to live a life of luxury, or do you want to do something altruistic with it? What would make you happiest?" He smiled at her. "There's no wrong answer."

"I kind of feel like there is, though," said Peach. "When you ask it like that, I feel like there's no way I can say I want to keep even a single cent of the money for myself."

Dan raised his eyebrows. "Seriously? You can't make others happy until you're happy yourself. Do you own your own home, Ms. Trimble? Do you have a healthcare plan in place?"

Peach pouted. "Isn't this a conversation for my financial advisor?"

"You can only be advised about how to use your finances when we figure out what you want. I promise you, nobody's going to call you selfish if you want to make plans to spend all of this money on yourself. Look at Isaac. He's built this empire. Do you think *he's* selfish?" Dan gestured around the luxurious Mediterranean-style mansion, then out of the window, toward the rest of the compound.

"I never thought about it before, but... I guess he is," said Peach. She felt a sting of guilt in her gut as she said that. "But then, he bought me all this wonderful stuff this morning. So, maybe he's *not* selfish. He's too generous to be selfish. But maybe I could say he's... a consumer? And maybe you could say that consumers are... greedy?" She suddenly gasped as she remembered what had happened at the brasserie. "He's definitely uncharitable."

"You seem to be asking me a lot of questions," said Dan. "I'm the one here to ask you. I just want to help you realize. You're about to receive ten million dollars, Ms. Trimble. That's a life-changing amount of money. An overwhelming amount of money. It's important that this money brings you happiness. And for that to happen, we need to figure out what it is you want."

Peach took a few long, deep breaths, trying to steady herself.

What I want.

What do I want?

She'd spent so many years volunteering at the rescue center, giving back to the community, that she'd gotten carried away with the luxury and glamor that Isaac's company had offered her. But she knew, deep down, that in the long term, she'd want more.

"I need an ambition," she said quietly. "Something big. Like I used to have, back when I was a little girl."

Dan grinned. "What did you used to want? When you were a little girl?"

"Before I worked at the animal rescue center," Peach said, "I wanted to *own* one."

"Now there's something for us to think about," said Dan, scribbling a bunch of notes down on the paper with excitement.

Peach felt excitement running through her too. But along with that excitement, she felt fear. Because she knew, deep down, that Isaac couldn't be part of her big plan. Isaac Righton was a sexy, rich, demanding Daddy. But... he hated animals. And he maybe hated charity too. He definitely wasn't the sort of man who would spend all his money on a pet rescue center... And Peach was. It was time for her to do some real good in this world.

Chapter Fifteen

ISAAC

WAKING UP ON THE morning of his wedding, Isaac decided that his Alaskan-sized bed had never felt bigger. Or lonelier.

Why had he bought such a huge mattress when he lived all by himself?

And, more to the point, why had Peach told him that she wanted to spend the night at her place last night?

He knew that the brunch with Daisy and Kiera had gone badly. And he felt terribly guilty about that. But aside from that, they'd had a wonderful morning together. He'd made her come for the first time. Then *he'd* come all over her beautiful body and made her breakfast in bed. He'd bought her some of the sexiest, cutest luxury items that Bal Harbor had to offer. He'd fed her so many pancakes she looked fit to burst.

What had gone wrong?

He had hoped that she'd have been fired up by the time he returned home from work last night. She'd had a meeting with a life coach, which he hoped would have been positive for her. As her Daddy, her fiancé, and her benefactor, it was important to him that she felt good about the money she was about to receive. That she had a plan in place for how she'd like to use it.

They'd had fun at the mall, of course, but retail therapy wasn't the be-all-and-end-all — far from it. Isaac knew better than anyone that money didn't cure all your problems. And having a lot of it in your pocket but no damn idea what to spend it all on, actually made you kinda miserable.

That's why he'd loved taking Peach to the mall, actually. And having her in his life in general. It felt so good buying her things. To be a giver, not just a receiver, for once.

Last night, though, she'd told him she'd needed some space.

And he respected that.

It just felt really fucking lonely without her.

Miiiiiaow!

"Alright, Itchy," said Isaac, looking down at the kitten trying to jump up onto his mattress. "I guess I'm not alone with you here."

Itchy gave up trying to climb onto the bed and started chasing its tail instead.

"You really are a silly thing," Isaac said, surprised by how tender his voice was when speaking to the creature. Bit by bit, the animal had grown on him. He had stopped chasing up his PA to find a home for it. Had started to accept that maybe, just maybe, this was his life now. He was... a cat person.

"Oh dear, Itchy," he said. "I think that girl is making me soft. I'm talking to animals now."

Itchy paid him no attention whatsover, and continued chasing his tail.

Isaac got out of bed and checked his watch. Three hours until the wedding. Montague and Bastion were due over in a while. His best men. They still weren't happy about the wedding, but they were going along with it.

Before they arrived, Isaac would need a shower and a shave. He just didn't feel like showering or shaving right now though. He wanted to see *her*. He had a few gifts to give her, but really, the gifts were kind of an excuse. He needed to talk to her.

He gathered his stuff together and headed for Peach's mansion. As he pressed the doorbell, he felt nervous all of a sudden. Like he was a teenager again, waiting to see if the girl he liked wanted to go out with him.

Finally, she answered the door, and his anxiety didn't dissipate. If anything, it got worse.

She looked a-*ma*-zing.

She was wearing an open pink satin dressing gown, with a white nightie underneath. The fabric of the nightie was so thin it was almost see-through. He could make out her coral-colored nipples and her panties too. She wasn't wearing the special bridal underwear he'd bought her. In fact, he could make out her bare pussy, with that lick of blond hair at the top of it. His cock tightened.

"Isaac," she said with a rigid smile. It felt strange to hear him calling her that, and not "Daddy".

"Peach," he said awkwardly. "Can I come in?"

Peach nodded. "Of course."

She led him into the kitchen and he was surprised by how tidy it looked. Not perfect, but nothing like the mess he'd seen last time he was here.

He set down his leather briefcase on the countertop and took a seat on the stool beside it. "I have some things for you," he said.

"Isn't it bad luck to see me the morning of the wedding?" Peach asked.

"Doesn't feel very unlucky," Isaac said with a smile. "Feels quite the opposite, actually."

Peach didn't smile back. She looked strangely terrified.

"Darling," he said, "you know, if you're having second thoughts, I completely understand. I know I got you to sign a bunch of paperwork, but there *was* a get-out clause in there. If the idea of marrying me is making you unhappy, then—"

"No," Peach said quickly. "It's not that."

Isaac inwardly sighed with relief. "Then what is it, cupcake?"

"It's..." Peach wrung her hands. "It's just what happens afterward."

Isaac tried to read her expression. Was she worried about him leaving her? Or was she worried that he wouldn't want to leave?

"Babygirl," he said, "all this stuff that's happened between us... it's been very quick and very intense..." He felt his lips grow dry. "But for me, it's been a blast. No. That makes it sound unimportant. It's been... *life-changing.*"

Peach didn't look horrified by that idea, but she didn't look overjoyed either.

"Look," Isaac said, "it's important you know that you're in control here. In terms of our relationship *and* our marriage."

Peach bit her thumbnail. "In control how?"

"Well obviously, in a Dom-sub relationship, there's an illusion that the Dom is the one who holds all the power. But deep down, it's the sub who's in control. You set the limits. As your Dom, I'm here to serve you. If what you want is for a man to take control in the bedroom, that's what you get. But only if you want it. And only for as long as you want it."

Peach nodded. "Okay."

"And as for the marriage... If you're feeling weird about the idea of a fake wedding, we don't have to do it, you know. I'd completely understand." He took a deep breath. "In fact, if you want to have a *real* relationship and ditch the wedding, then I'm up for that."

Peach suddenly looked pale. "I'm just... not sure..."

Isaac nodded. "I think I get it now. You want to get married but you're not sure about our relationship?"

Peach's cheeks turned crimson. "I don't know. It's not that I don't like you, Da— I mean, Isaac. I just have to think about how my life is going to change after we... after I get..."

Isaac stood up. "Sweetheart. I understand totally. Honestly. I promise. I'm offering you a huge sum of money. That's a once-in-a-lifetime opportunity to do something big. There's no reason why I should factor into your plans. We've only known each other five minutes. Like I said, you're in control. And I respect your decision — whatever it is."

"Thank you," said Peach, wiping definite tears from her eyes. "I just... The life coach said... Never mind. It's all good. I appreciate you coming to talk to me."

He opened up his leather satchel and began taking out a variety of objects. "On the subject of luck, I brought you a variety of objects which I hope will make you very lucky indeed."

He lined them up before her.

Something old: a brooch with a picture of a horse on it.

"It was my mother's," he told her. "She loved horses."

Something new: a white handkerchief with "Peach Trimble" embroidered on it in pink.

"I thought you might like something with your true name on it. You'll be Peach Righton for a while, until the marriage is annulled. This is just a little reminder for you of who you really are inside."

Something borrowed: a pocket book from Miami-Dade Public Library entitled: Fairytales for Girls.

"I thought I could read them to you at bedtime," said Isaac. "If you want to share a bed, that is."

"These are wonderful," she blurted. "That's so kind of you."

"I've been saving the best until last," he told her. "Something blue." He looked around. "Where's Teddy?"

She pointed to a scruffy little heap in the corner, and he became aware of the sound of Teddy snoring.

"Ah," he said. "When he wakes up, you can give this to him." He took a small blue bow tie out of the bag.

Peach burst out laughing. "Wow. He's going to look so freaking cute in that thing! And it's okay. You can put it on him now if you like."

Isaac suddenly felt like this was a test. He'd walked Teddy on a leash yesterday, but now Peach was asking him to touch him. A week ago, he'd never have done it with his allergies. But today, he was going to give it a try.

He took the bow tie over to Teddy, and, carefully, he tied it around his neck. His eyes itched a little, but he survived. So did Teddy, by the looks of it. He cast Isaac a lazy look and then settled back down to sleep again. The bow tie looked perfect on him. Funny, cute, and charming, all at once.

"Hey," said Peach. "You didn't even sneeze."

Isaac grinned. "I got a shot yesterday. It's one of the things I was busy with after I left you. I started a course of immunotherapy. Felt like it was about time I dealt with my allergies."

Peach put her hand to her mouth. "You did that for me?"

Isaac shrugged. "Well, for you and for Teddy. And for furry creatures everywhere, I guess."

Peach looked over at Teddy, then up at Isaac. "So... you don't hate animals?" Isaac shook his head. "No. Of course not. I'm just wary of them. Been hard to get close to them seeing as they literally make me ill."

Peach nodded. "That makes sense. I'd be wary too if I had allergies." She had an excited glint in her eye now, and he couldn't help but notice that her nipples had grown hard beneath the sheer fabric of her nightie.

"Young lady," he said, "are you thinking naughty thoughts?"

"That depends," Peach replied. "Have I got time to be thinking naughty thoughts?"

Isaac looked at his watch. Damn. Montague and Bastion were due over to his place any minute.

"I think you're gonna have to hold those thoughts," he said, as his cock swelled uncontrollably, trying to tempt him to change his mind. "You won't forget to wear that special lingerie I got for you, will you?"

"No, Daddy," Peach replied. "I won't forget a thing."

*

Peach looked good enough to eat. A pink wedding dress with frills and lacy bit and bows, all of which showed off her incredible curves and voluptuous figure.

Isaac had written special vows for them, and it felt great saying them to her, even if their marriage was only to be a short one.

"I promise to be a faithful husband," he'd said, "and a good Daddy. I promise to cherish you and punish you in just the right quantities. To guide you and be guided by you every day that we're together."

Even though they were in public, in the bar, surrounded by friends, it had been almost impossible to stop himself from getting hard. He just found the idea of getting married so damn wonderful. And getting married to *her*: a dream come true. He couldn't help fantasizing constantly about pushing his Little wife over the table and claiming her as his partner today and forevermore.

Which was exactly what he wasn't allowed to do.

Still, it felt good to pretend. Cindy had decorated the bar beautifully for them. Bunting made of pink and white teddy bears. Pink loveheart fairy lights and a pink neon sign saying "Daddy and Babygirl". And it had all felt so magical. Seeing Teddy bring in their wedding rings on a little cushion attached to his back. Saying their vows. Cutting into their decadent red velvet chocolate cake together once the party started. Having their first dance: "Baby I'm Yours" by the Arctic Monkeys.

It all felt so... real.

And so... right.

Well, obviously there were some issues. Daisy looked upset the whole way through the ceremony. Montague looked exhausted. Kiera looked combative. Bastion looked drunk. But the main thing was, Peach looked happy. And he felt on top of the damn world.

"Mrs. Righton," Isaac whispered into Peach's ear as they bumped into one another outside the bathroom.

"Mr. Righton," Peach giggled. Her face was flushed after a glass of champagne and he made a mental note to watch she didn't drink anymore. Emotions were high between them today. He wanted this to be a day to remember for Peach, not a day she looked back on with embarrassment.

"Come with me," he commanded, taking her by the hand and leading her to the back room behind the pub that Cindy had set up for them. A place for the bride and groom to retreat when they needed a moment alone.

"Is this our secret love nest, Daddy?" Peach asked, laughing, as they entered the room. There was a dog bed for Teddy in there, and a little bunk in case Peach wanted to take a nap, plus some toys and stuffies in case she needed time in Little Space. "Wow," she said as she saw it. "You really thought of everything."

"Sweetheart," said Isaac, turning to her. "I did it all for you! He looked around, checking there was nobody lurking outside the room, eavesdropping. "I know this marriage isn't—" he whispered the next word, "—*real*. But I want the day to feel special for you. For us."

Peach nodded. "It does feel special, Daddy."

Isaac smiled. "I like that you're calling me Daddy again."

She grinned. "I like that your Daddy parts are getting hard around me again."

He looked down at his crotch, noticing the swelling. "That never stopped, babygirl," he said, taking her hand — the one with the gold wedding band on it — and pressing it against his hot, hard erection. "You know, I never wanted you more than right now. Seeing you in that frilly pink wedding dress. My wife."

"My husband," Peach said, letting him guide her hand up and down his shaft, still trapped behind his pants.

"So... are you going to let Daddy see that bridal lingerie he bought you?" Peach pretended to look shocked. "Is *that* why you booked out this private back room, Daddy? Because you wanted someplace secret to see my panties?"

"That's one of the reasons," Isaac admitted, opening the top button of his fly and pushing Peach's hand all the way inside his boxers, letting her fingertips rub over the engorged tip of his cock, already seeping with precum. Then, he removed Peach's hand and placed it on the hem of her dress. In a deep, confident voice, he said: "Show me your panties, Little girl."

Peach's eyes sparkled as she lifted the hem of her wedding dress.

Isaac watched in delight as Peach took the dress off completely, and her lingerie set was revealed to him in full. The bra was stunning. Silky white, with slits on the breasts, letting the perfect pink rosebuds of her nipples poke temptingly through. But the panties... they were white too, with "Just Married" written inside a pink heart on the front. Just below the heart, he could make out the start of the opening in the panties. He had picked these out specially.

"Turn around," he ordered.

Slowly, she spun around for him, revealing her beautiful, round bottom. The opening in the panties went all the way up past her butt. Crotchless, buttless panties. He had never seen anything more delightful.

"Damn, woman," he growled. "I knew these would look good on you, but..."

"They feel very naughty, Daddy," said Peach, shifting her weight from foot to foot, making her ass cheeks squish and stretch around in all kinds of mesmerizing ways. "I've been getting very wet wearing them."

"I'll bet you have," said Isaac. "Thank you for telling me, sweetheart. Now I want you to bend over and show Daddy."

"Show you how wet I am?"

"Mm-hmm." Isaac reached inside his pants, stroking his hard-on as Peach walked over to the bunk, climbing onto it on all fours and parting her legs for him. He stood behind her and took a good look. Her pussy wasn't just glistening for him — it was *flowing*. A long, clear line of moisture hung between her legs, and the insides of her thighs were slick with lust.

Holy shit.

"I can't help it, Daddy," Peach said, embarrassed. "I hope you don't think it's too much..."

"Too much?" said Isaac, his voice strained. "There's no such thing as too wet, sugarplum. And Daddy would really love nothing more than to plunge his dick deep inside that tight fountain—"

"I know, I know," Peach said, looking back at him. "We can't because of the annulment. But I'm guessing there's a reason why you got me these buttless panties? For, um, easy back access? I'm guessing it'll be alright if we...?"

"Only if you want me to," Isaac said carefully. "You know it's what I want, babygirl. You know I want it all."

Peach appeared to be panting. Her pussy started to drip even more now. "I want it all too, Daddy."

"You do?"

"Mm-hmm." Peach's hand traveled up between her thighs, her fingers hovering just an inch below her soaking pussy. "Would it be okay if I touched myself? While you put your thing in my bottom, Daddy?"

Isaac looked down at his "thing", so hard and hungry he could hardly speak. Then he looked back at *her*. Her everything. "Daddy wants to be the one to touch you," he said, climbing onto the bunk behind her. He released his cock fully from his pants, and held it against one of her butt cheeks, feeling her warmth.

His heart was racing. Here he was, in bed with his new wife. Their private parts legally belonging to one another. His cock and her cunt, naked and almost touching. Feeling the heat rising off one another. Ready to seal the deal.

His fingers stroked her soft tummy, then played with her clit for a moment. Then, he slid his middle finger deep into her hole, wet and tight and exactly as he wanted it to feel. He took his finger out of her again, bringing it to his mouth and sucking it, tasting her.

"I want..." he groaned, his cock rubbing against her buttock. "I want to fuck you..."

"But we can't, Daddy," said Peach, sticking her ass out and upward so that her moist slit was stroking the base of his dick. "You said it would make things too complicated."

He moved his hips back and forth, massaging his cock up and down her wet opening. "Maybe complicated isn't so bad," he told her. "Maybe complicated is worth it."

He could feel Peach shuddering beneath him now and he made an executive decision. Screw it. It was only legal fees and a little extra paperwork. The hassle was worth it if he got to claim her. His sweet Little wifey. Mrs. Peach Righton. His plump, tasty, juicy darling. He pushed down on the base of her spine, pressing her tummy against the mattress. Then, he flipped her over.

"If I'm going to do it, then I'm going to make sure that it's *me* who's doing all the doing," he said. "This is my fault, and mine only. Understood?"

Peach nodded, placing her arms above her head as he was showing her.

He pinned down her arms with one hand and pressed his thighs down hard on hers. She was completely at his mercy. Other than her safeword, she had no escape from this.

"Daddy's going to make you his wife properly now," he said, looking her square in the eye.

"Okay, Daddy," she whispered, her hips squirming in anticipation.

With his free hand, he grabbed hold of his cock, which was in such a heightened state of arousal that he had to remind himself not to come instantly, then he guided it carefully down to her pussy. Slipping around slightly in her slick juices, he forced his dick to her entrance, and slowly, wetly, he squeezed into her.

Her pussy tightened around him, and then relaxed.

"Good girl," he said. "Remember to keep breathing."

Still pinning her down so hard he wondered if he'd leave marks on her wrists, he began to fuck her now. Long, deep thrusts, making sure that his cock went into the very depths of her. His balls pushed up against her ample ass cheeks as he slid into her center. With each new thrust, he watched her breasts jiggle. He sucked her hard nipples, loving how they shone with his spit.

As for her pussy... it felt divine. It felt like he belonged in it. It felt like it was her wedding gift to him. A gift that he wanted to keep taking and taking, *for as long as they both shall live...*

He knew how wrong this was. He knew she didn't want to be with him forever. And yet he couldn't help it. He was completely addicted her. When he was with her, he was her Daddy. It couldn't be any other way. And the thought of her ever fucking anyone else drove him wild with jealousy. He had to claim her, right now, to let her know that she was his.

His fingers sought out her clit, determined to make her climax just as strong as his. He could feel how close he was, and he needed to bring her to the edge with him. To make her take that leap off the cliff edge with him. A leap into the unknown. A leap into pleasure like they'd never felt before.

Her legs trembled beneath his. Her spine arched and her eyes rolled back. She was close too. He needed to bring her closer. He bent down, kissing her full on the lips, his tongue dancing with hers, guiding her toward happy oblivion. She moaned and groaned, and he moaned with her. They were one at last, moving together like there was no way to tell where one of them ended and the other began. And it was in that moment, the moment where he was her and she was him, that he brought them both to climax. Loud, earth-shattering, and so fucking intense he thought they both might just explode.

As his cock spurted out endless gouts of hot cum deep inside her, he felt her pussy throb and spasm around him. He pushed his dick all the way in and held it there for as long as possible, wanting to bathe in their fuck fluids for as long as possible.

Fuck fluids.

A phrase like that should have been vulgar or disgusting. With her, it was pure heaven. With her, he felt dirtier and *Daddier* than ever before.

Breathing heavily, sweat pricking her skin, she looked up at him. "Daddy," she panted, fluttering her eyelashes. "That felt magical."

He bent down and kissed her tenderly, stroking her hair, moving his spent cock inside her just enough to elicit a final few throbs from her pussy.

"It's not over until you want it to be, darling," he whispered in her ear.

Even as he said those words, he knew the weight of them. Knew that he was promising that he was hers for as long as she liked.

"I need to give you something now, though," he told her, finally peeling himself away from her, trying not to look at her voluptuous figure, peeping out of that lingerie, for fear that he'd grow hard and have to take her again before she was ready.

"You already gave me so much," she giggled, keeping her legs parted wide, the cum spilling out of her a touch already, dribbling down onto the freshly-made bed.

"This is important," he said to her, reaching for an envelope on the table beside the bed. He'd placed this here in preparation earlier. It was the whole reason he'd brought her into the back room. He hadn't meant to fuck her. He never should have done it. But he was never going to regret it as long as he lived.

Peach took the envelope and opened it, half-smiling in anticipation. "Is it a wedding card?"

The moment she saw what was inside, her expression changed. Multiple emotions seemed to flash in her eyes all at once: surprise, excitement, disappointment. She closed her legs, sitting up straight. "It's a check for five million dollars."

"The other five will be with you after the annulment," he said helpfully, worried that she was disappointed that the full amount wasn't there.

"Oh, it's not that," she said. "It's just... so... final, I guess. Feels kinda like severance pay."

"There's something else in there too," he said, trying to cheer her up.

She fished inside the envelope and pulled out a key. "What's this for?"

"It's a key to the third mansion in my compound. I'm calling it the Honeymoon Suite." He smiled. "Shall we meet there in an hour?"

Her eyes widened. "I don't know what you're up to, Daddy, but I like the sound of it." She let her legs fall open again.

"I hope you're not too full of wedding cake," he told her, looking at her with yearning desire, "because Daddy has plans to put you on a heavy diet of cock and cum for the next few days."

"I have plenty of room for those things," she said, giggling.

*

"Thank you for a great party," Isaac told Montague and Bastion. "I'm going to meet Peach back at our place now. Get the honeymoon started."

"You look like you got the honeymoon started already," said Bastion, gesturing at Isaac's ruffled clothes. "Disappearing with the bride in the back room just now. You know she's too young for you, Isaac. She'll bleed you dry and then leave you for a younger model."

Poor Bastion. He still hadn't gotten over his ex leaving him. He'd half-wondered if something was going to happen between him and Kiera today. They were both miserable, angry people by the looks of it. But every time he saw them anywhere near each other they seemed to be arguing. Never mind. Bastion would find his Forever Girl. And she'd be a helluva lot less grumpy than Kiera, hopefully.

"If she leaves me then I'll be grateful I at least got to claim her once," Isaac said, with more truth behind those words than his friends knew.

"Ha," Bastion laughed glumly. "You've got it bad."

Montague wasn't responding to either of them. He kept looking over at Daisy glumly, and she kept shaking her head scornfully at him.

"You alright, dude?" Isaac asked Montague. "You know I'm going to look after Peach, right? I'll treat her like a princess."

"It's not that," said Montague. "I'm not thrilled about how fast you and Peach got together. But I know you're the kind of guy that sees an opportunity and goes for it. I get it. Peach is a cutie. Not sure Daisy feels the same. She's protective over her friend."

"I get that," said Isaac. "I'll prove to her, over time, that I'm not here to cause Peach any hurt."

"It's Daisy's hurt you need to make amends for," said Montague.

"Huh?" Isaac didn't follow. "You know we were getting married at a secret venue?" Montague asked.

"Yeah..."

"It was meant to be this place. This is where Daisy and I first met. We asked Cindy to keep it a secret, which is why I'm guessing she couldn't tell you."

Oh, fuck. Daisy was mad because Isaac and Peach had stolen her venue. Not to mention gotten married before her. Not that it was a competition, but it probably felt like they'd stolen the limelight.

"I'm sorry," said Isaac. "None of this was meant to hurt you or Daisy."

Bastion grunted drunkenly from the sidelines. "Marriage always ends up hurting someone," he slurred.

"I just hope you're marrying her for the right reasons," Montague said, placing a hand on Isaac's shoulder. "By which I mean for love. Not just to get in her panties."

"Too late for that," scoffed Bastion.

"Of course I'm marrying her for the right reasons," Isaac said. Though even as he said the words, he felt plagued by guilt and doubt. *The right reasons.*

Still. It was done now. And he did have reasons for the marriage. Even if Montague wouldn't have seen them as the right ones.

*

"Aunt Meg?" he said into his cell phone as he stood outside the bar. "Guess what?"

Aunt Meg gave a hacking cough, then, with about as much interest as a pig had in taking a bath, she said: "What?"

He took a deep breath, then, enjoying the phrase immensely, he said: "I'm married."

There was a brief pause, and then Aunt Meg burst out laughing. Finally, she composed herself. "Well, guess what?" she said in return. "I put the ranch on the market yesterday, and it's already been sold."

Isaac swallowed. *No. This can't be true.* "For how much?"

His aunt snorted. "Five million dollars."

Chapter Sixteen

PEACH

IMAGINE BEING SO RICH you could make an entire mansion into a honeymoon suite.

And yet... Peach had five million dollars. She *was* rich enough to own a mansion. It was a funny feeling. But she guessed, if she was going to give the money to charity, that it didn't make her rich.

So why was it that she kept being so attracted to Isaac's wealth? Was it so wrong of her? She'd spent all those years living in squalor, with barely a cent to her name, scraping by on shitty scraps of food, wearing clothes she'd had for a million years. Was it *so* bad to enjoy a little luxury?

She and Teddy stepped into the mansion, her heart racing.

According to tradition, Isaac should have carried her over the threshold into this place. But their wedding had been anything but traditional. And there was something quite exciting about going in here on her own, to discover what Isaac had set up for her. Then waiting for him to come find her.

What had happened between them at the bar was unexpected. She was a tangle of contradictions right now. She knew that she needed to do the right thing once the money was in her bank. And that Isaac probably wouldn't support her actions. She was preparing herself for the fact their marriage was getting annulled. Trying to protect herself from the disappointment of that by convincing herself that Isaac wasn't right for her in the first place.

But... getting married today. It just felt so freaking special. It felt even more special than that. It was the best day of her entire life. Seeing him in that tux. Saying those beautiful vows to her. Dancing with him. Her *husband*. And then, wearing that naughty underwear while he made her his.

She shuddered just thinking about it. Her pussy ached for him. Her heart longed for him. It was just her head that told her to slow the heck down.

But now that she was entering the honeymoon mansion, her heart was telling her head to eff off all over again. He'd thought of everything. The wedding venue had been decorated in pink, but this place was all red. Red petals strewn across the floor, leading up the enormous staircase in swirling, inviting patterns. As she followed them, she passed ice sculptures of swans with red gems pressed into them, their necks bowed into the shape of hearts. She saw red balloons and red candles and more red roses than she could count.

"What do you think, Teddy?" she asked. "Pretty nice, eh?"

The wedding had been decorated like a wedding for show, but this place was just for them. So why had Isaac gone so overboard? If the wedding was fake, then the honeymoon was entirely unnecessary. Unless he really did like her...

She couldn't allow herself to entertain that thought, though. She knew he'd been a good Daddy to her. That he'd taken responsibility for her welfare while their agreement was in place. But deep down, she really was just Peach Trimble. The poor girl from the bad part of town. Plump and plain and kind of silly. And Isaac was... Isaac. A buff billionaire. Able to sleep with whoever he wanted, whenever he wanted, in whatever damn way he wanted.

Most likely, she was a novelty for him. An overweight girl with a funny accent and a bad education. Maybe he was checking off a box: fucking Cinderella. And maybe she was checking off a box too: doing it with the handsome Prince.

It's just... it had felt like so much more than that.

She climbed the staircase all the way to the top, with Teddy following right behind. This mansion wasn't as full of personality as hers, and it wasn't as grand as his, but it was dripping with potential. Amazing views of the ocean out of just about every window. Wide open spaces and incredible details. She had visions of how exciting it would be to turn it into something together. A project for them. A family home.

Did she really just think that?

She followed the rose petals into a grand bedroom and discovered a large four-poster bed with rose petals scattered onto it in the shape of a heart. This man really had gone all out on the wedding night fantasy. And for one night only, she wanted to go along with that fantasy too.

"Don't look, Teddy," she whispered.

But Teddy had already found a sunny spot by the window, and he curled up happily, going straight to sleep. It always amazed her how quickly and easily he did that.

Peach stood in front of the bed, peeling off her clothes, including her underwear. She let it all drop to the floor. She considered finding a bathroom and taking a shower, but she could still smell his aftershave on her skin, and she liked that. She could feel his cum seeping out from between her legs too. She liked that even more. She climbed onto the bed, lying naked on the rose petals, sighing deeply.

"What's a girl to do?"

She looked up at the high ceiling, with a huge ceiling rose and chandelier in the center, and she allowed herself to enjoy this.

She wasn't meant to touch herself without her Daddy's permission, but surely just this once he wouldn't mind? They'd gotten married today. He'd told her to wait for him here. He'd made the place more romantic than Paris. Surely he had this in mind for her.

She gently sucked her finger, then trailed it down her nipple, her belly, her pubic mound. She touched her clit, rubbing her own moisture onto it. She closed her eyes, wriggling and gasping as the passion overtook her. Her plan was to make herself come as many times as she possibly could before Isaac returned...

But she didn't even manage it once.

"Hey," he said, walking into the room, barely looking at her. He sat on the edge of the bed and sighed.

Peach squealed and jerked her hand away from her pussy, embarrassed at being caught. "It's not what it looks like, Daddy," she panted, crawling under the covers and pulling them up to her neck. "I was just feeling for my IUD. Checking it was in place."

Still, Isaac seemed to hardly notice her. "It didn't work. The plan didn't work. This whole thing has been a disaster."

A disaster.

Peach didn't know what Isaac was talking about exactly, but his words stung. Was that how he saw *her*? A disaster?

He reached into the inside of his jacket pocket and threw down two plane tickets on the mattress. "We were meant to be going here for our honeymoon. Tickets to Europe. A luxury cruise, starting in Spain." He looked at her, his hard eyes softening slightly. "Twiddly music, pink drinks, and juicy oranges. That's what you said you liked, didn't you?"

"A honeymoon in Europe?" Peach said, her eyes wide. She'd told him early on that she'd always wanted to go. That's one of the reasons he let her stay in his Mediterranean-inspired mansion. But this gesture... a honeymoon in Europe... it was beyond romantic. Or at least, it would have been... if it didn't sound like he was trying to tell her that it was all over.

"It's very kind of you," said Peach, trying not to sound disappointed, "but honestly, don't worry about it. It sounds like you've gone off the idea." She paused for a moment. "I have plans anyway."

He frowned. "You do?"

"Yeah," she said, unable to hide her smile. "I cashed in that check on the way here. I kinda already spent it, you see."

"Already?"

"Uh-huh," she said. "The life coach you got me encouraged me to act quick."

Isaac looked impressed. He turned to her, taking hold of her feet under the covers and giving them a loving stroke. "What are you buying with it?"

"Oh," said Peach shrugging, "it's just... an animal thing."

"You're buying a five-million-dollar animal? Must be pretty rare," Isaac joked half-heartedly.

"No," said Peach. Her cheeks were burning now. "It's something you won't approve of. Being an animal hater. And a charity hater too."

Isaac stopped stroking her feet. "What are you talking about? An animal hater? A charity hater? What kind of guy do you think I am?"

"I'm setting up my own pet rescue center," Peach blurted. "I just bought the perfect bit of land for it." She grabbed her purse from the floor and got out her cell phone. "Look," she said. "It's an old ranch. A few hours away from here. A real mess. Falling apart at the seams. But I can rip the place down and start again."

Peach looked at Isaac, and saw that his face was white as a ghost.

Chapter Seventeen

ISAAC

"**Y**OU CAN'T HAVE IT," Isaac snapped, his heart racing. "You have to cancel the sale. Now."

He ran his hand through his hair, trying to find a way to calm down. He couldn't let Peach buy his family home. The land that his parents were buried on.

Peach glared at him. "I knew you'd hate the idea. Helping animals. Running a charity. It's obvious that you disapprove. I bet you got me that life coach and financial adviser because you wanted me to spend all my money on, I don't know, stocks and shares or something."

"Stocks and shares?" replied Isaac. "What are you talking about? You can spend that money however you like. Just... not on that ranch."

Peach huffed, pulling the covers around herself. "You just think I'm a silly little girl, don't you?"

Isaac reached out toward her, but she edged away. "No. Of course I don't. I think you're an incredible, amazing woman. But I'm not sure that you like *me* very much."

Peach looked at him with those big blue eyes. He longed to be able to jump under the covers with her, to slide his cock deep inside her, to celebrate their marriage in all kinds of bold, beautiful ways. But by the looks of it, she didn't feel the same way. After all the effort he'd made, all the ways he'd tried to show her that he was a good guy, she still seemed to think he was a grade-A dick.

Maybe she had been pretending to like him. Playing along until she got his money. Now, he was starting to see how she really felt. He just wished she hadn't let him fuck her, though. He had gotten way too carried away. His heart was raw and vulnerable, and now it felt like she was crushing it with her bare hands.

Well, screw it. What did it matter? She'd got what she wanted.

But he wasn't giving up the ranch.

"That ranch," he said, through gritted teeth, "is mine."

Peach looked confused. "No," she said, "it's mine."

Isaac closed his eyes and took a deep breath. "It's my family ranch," he explained. "You can buy literally any ranch except that one."

Peach's hand flew to her mouth. "It's yours?"

"Yes. It's my home."

Peach's cheeks burned bright red. "That's crazy... How did that even... But wait." She looked at him. "I thought you said the plan didn't work. Does that mean your aunt doesn't want you to have it?"

"I spoke to her on the phone half an hour ago. She told me she never thought I'd really get married. Then she laughed. Said I was a fool. Said she—" he gritted his teeth, "—pitied the fool who agreed to marry me."

Peach reached for *his* hand now, but he pulled away. "The thing is, though, Isaac..."

There it was again. His first name. Not "Daddy" or "sir" or any of the other names that made his heart flutter.

"The thing is," she said again, "your aunt says you can't have the ranch. So if I don't buy it, then won't it go to some stranger?"

Isaac narrowed his eyes. "You're saying I have to let you buy my ranch and tear it down and build a pet rescue center on it because the other option is even worse?"

Peach's jaw dropped. She gestured around the room. "Look at all this. You have everything. And you want to buy your family ranch *why*? So you can build a hotel on it? As an investment? Don't you think you have enough stuff? Why don't you sell it to a good cause?"

"I see what you think of me," said Isaac, standing up. "You think I'm a greedy asshole who wants to build some kind of evil empire, all to make more money."

Peach jumped out of bed, taking the blankets with her. "And I see what you think of *me*. Some silly little airhead who wants to give away all your hard-earned money to charity. And to an *animal* charity at that. I just wish..."

"What?" barked Isaac. "What do you wish?"

"I wish I'd never met you!" Peach yelled.

Isaac's blood was boiling. "The feeling's mutual."

Just then, Teddy woke up and started yapping furiously at him. That screeching bark was more than Isaac would take right now.

"I'm leaving," he said. "You and your dog have exactly one hour to vacate my property."

With that, he walked out.

And as he did, his heart felt like it shattered into a million tiny pieces.

Chapter Eighteen

PEACH

P EOPLE ALWAYS SAID THAT money didn't buy you happiness.

Ten million dollars.

Peach had money coming out of her ears.

And what people said was right. The money wasn't making her happy at all. The money had led to her losing all her friends. Losing the man she had called Daddy. Losing her old life back in Connecticut.

Now, she was driving a hire car, traveling toward a ranch that wasn't rightfully hers, wondering how things had gotten so messed up.

She had tried calling Daisy and Kiera, hoping to confess the whole sorry story to them. How hurt she'd been when Kiera had decided to move to Miami. How jealous she'd been of them both, and how she'd agreed to this stupid marriage pact as a way of trying to feel good about herself.

But Daisy was too sad to talk to her right now. Apparently, she'd ruined Daisy's wedding by booking the venue that Daisy was meant to get married in. Daisy was taking it personally, assuming that Peach had done it on purpose somehow. A punishment for leaving Connecticut and convincing Kiera to go with her.

She knew that because Kiera *was* talking to her. But Kiera was using a lot of angry words. She told Peach that she'd been "freaked out" by her behavior lately. That it seemed like Peach was "acting up" by marrying Isaac. Trying to "prove a point" to them by marrying someone who was "totally wrong" for her. She even cussed a couple times. Said that she cared about Peach, that she loved her, but that she needed some time to cool off before they could hang out properly again.

Peach told Kiera that she could explain everything, but Kiera didn't reply. Peach would have to wait.

It sucked, to be honest, that her best friends weren't more supportive of her marriage. Even though she'd messed up by inadvertently stealing Daisy's wedding venue, her friends could have at least tried to be there for her a bit more. She had gotten married! That was huge! Not only that, but, for a while at least, she'd actually *liked* Isaac. Their marriage had felt... real.

Ah well. Her friends didn't care about her, and neither did Isaac.

Now, she was doing the only thing that she *could* do. She was following through on a plan. Trying to make something of herself, because otherwise... there was nothing.

Teddy was in a carrier in the back of the car and they were heading to the ranch.

"I know what you're thinking Teddy," Peach called back to her little dog. "You think I'm mean. But if Isaac can't have that ranch, then isn't it better that *I* have it instead of some, some... property developer?"

Teddy didn't respond. He was asleep, most likely.

Peach kept her eyes on the road, but her heart was in her throat. None of this felt right. It felt like she was sneaking around behind Isaac's back. Stealing from him.

Obviously, she'd thought about buying Isaac's ranch and then giving it to him. But that was risky. Because if she did that, and he just took it from her, she'd lost five million dollars. And she got the feeling that she'd be lucky to see the other five million he said he'd pay her. Sure, they'd signed a contract... but then they'd broken the terms of it. They'd consummated the marriage, which meant they could no longer get it annulled. Which meant that technically, he didn't have to pay her.

Oh, man. She'd been so foolish. That's probably why he'd done it. He'd slept with her so he didn't have to pay her the full amount.

And now he was trying to trick her into getting that first five million back by pretending that her ranch was his.

"When will I ever learn, Teddy?" she asked. "I'm too trusting. This whole arrangement was obviously too good to be true."

She began piecing it all together now. Remembering how Isaac had treated her that first time they met. Yelling "No animals" at her like she was nothing but dirt on the bottom of his shoe. This whole thing had probably been a ruse to humiliate her. Pretend to be into her. Pretend to be giving her ten million dollars. And at the same time, he could trick her to into buying his family ranch because he knew his aunt would never sell it to *him*.

Ugh, it all seemed so obvious now. The way that life coach had encouraged her to think big. To buy a big patch of land. He'd even been the one to open up the real estate website. The one that had the ranch for sale on it.

Silly, silly Peach. She should have stayed in her lane. The poor girl from Connecticut, sweeping up animal hair and working herself to the bone at the dog shelter. That was her destiny. As if *she* could have been a millionaire!

Except... she *did* have five million dollars.

And she *had* bought a ranch with it.

So if she *didn't* give the ranch to Isaac...

Maybe she had outsmarted him?

*

Mess everywhere. Old mattresses. Heaps of rotting rubbish. Thin, sick-looking cows. How on earth was this place worth five million?

"You seen enough yet?" snapped the old woman. She had been surprisingly unfriendly with Peach the whole time. You'd think she would have been delighted to meet the sucker who was paying her way too much money to take this dump off her hands.

Keep your eyes on the prize, Peach. It's not a matter of what this place is now. It's what it can become.

Of course, Peach worried that Isaac wasn't going to give her the next five million dollars. If he didn't give her the money, she wouldn't be able to do a single thing to this land. But she had to stay strong. She had to hope.

Even though the place was a mess, she could see its potential. The location was fantastic, near a beautiful river and a lake, but far enough inland that flooding wasn't a problem. There were nearly five-hundred acres of land — plenty for all the animals she hoped to have there. There were natural ponds for attracting teal ducks, and there was enough woodland for whitetail deer, Osceola turkeys, and wild boar. It was like she was buying her very own nature retreat. It was going to be heaven.

"I'd like to take a look around the back of the house," Peach said trying her best to sound authoritative. She didn't want this woman, Meg, to see how nervous she was.

"The back of the house? What do you want to see that for?" Meg spat. "It's just like the front... but it's the back."

Peach cleared her throat. "I'd like to check out the land behind it," she said. "To see if it would be good for some kennels."

"Kennels?" said Meg. "You're not a rancher then?"

"Um, no," said Peach, her heart racing. "I'm not exactly a rancher."

Meg stared at her, then shrugged. "Don't really care what you are as long as your money's good. But you've seen enough. I've got things to do."

Peach stood her ground. "I need to see the whole place. It's a big purchase, ma'am. I need to make sure I'm happy with it."

Meg narrowed her eyes. "You're not a serious buyer? You'd better not be wasting my time. Showing up here in your funny little outfit with your funny way of talking."

Peach looked down at her clothes: mint green overalls with cherries all over them. She'd worn them specially, thinking they gave a good impression. Ugh. She had so much to learn.

"Of course I'm serious, Ma'am," said Peach with a smile. "That's why I'm here. I just wanted to be one hundred percent, because I hadn't been able to see the place when I put in the offer—"

"If you're wasting my time, I'll just sell to someone else."

"No, please," said Peach. "I love it here. I just want to look round the back of the house."

Meg sighed, long and hard. "Fine. Come on then. Let's get it over with."

She walked around to the back of the house, with Peach following. As soon as they turned the corner, Peach was surprised to see two gravestones. They were covered in weeds, and there was yet another mattress dumped near them.

"Oh!" she said. "This is a graveyard?"

Meg shrugged defensively. "Just two of 'em. Dig them up if you like."

Peach stepped closer. She could make out the names on them. Deborah Maria Righton and William John Righton. They died within a week of one another.

Isaac's parents.

Instantly, tears filled Peach's eyes. She'd known it all along, of course: this place was rightfully his. No matter how hard she'd tried to justify herself, how big she'd allowed her dream to get, she couldn't have this place. She wouldn't be able to live with herself.

"I can't do this," Peach said softly.

"I knew it," Meg snapped. "I knew you weren't serious."

"No, I am, it's just... those graves... I..."

Could she tell Meg who she was? That she was Isaac's wife? Her bank account was still in her old name, so Meg had no idea.

"Whatever, missy," said the old woman. "You obviously have an aversion to buying land with... dead people... in it."

The way that Meg said *dead people...* it sent chills down Peach's spine.

"Anyway," said Meg, walking them around the front of the house. "I'll just sell this place to the second highest bidder. No big deal." She grinned. "He's planning on making the place into a slaughterhouse."

Peach's eyes widened. "No!"

She couldn't let that happen. She couldn't let Isaac's ranch turn into *that*.

"I'll buy it!" she blurted. She'd do what she'd always known was the right thing to do. She'd buy the ranch, and she'd give it to... "Isaac?"

At that very moment, Peach had just bumped into something hard and wide. Something fleshy and familiar. She looked up and saw him: her husband.

Isaac ignored Peach, looking at Meg in desperation.

"Please," Isaac begged her. "Aunt Meg. Don't sell the ranch to her. I'll pay twice what she's paying."

"Wait," said Meg, looking at Peach, and then back at Isaac. "How does she know you? She called you Isaac."

"She," said Isaac, with a deep breath, "is my wife."

"Your wife?" Meg said, taking a step back. "So, what's going on here? This was your Plan B? If I didn't sell it to you, you'd get your wife to trick me into selling it to her instead?"

"No," said Isaac, holding up his hands. "It's not like that. We're... we're actually getting a divorce. In fact, it's already in motion."

Peach felt a stab in her heart. It's not like she thought their relationship was headed anywhere other than this, but it hurt to hear Isaac talking about it so coldly. As if she wasn't here.

Meg waggled her finger first at Isaac, then at Peach. "And this is your Plan C, I presume? If all else fails, tell me you're getting a divorce? Try to get me to take pity on you, so I'll sell it to you, after all?"

"No," said Isaac, "it's not like that."

"Well, neither of you is buying it," said Meg. "I can tell you that much for certain. Now, get off my land or I'll call the cops."

Isaac looked at Peach with fury in his eyes, then he turned and marched off the land.

Peach had no choice but to follow him.

Chapter Nineteen

ISAAC

H E WAS MEANT TO be in Spain with her right now. Drinking sangria, listening to flamenco music, preparing for the luxury cruise of a lifetime.

Instead, she was following him down a single-track road in the middle of nowhere, as he drove away from the family home he'd never see again.

Plus, he was divorcing her.

The only woman he'd ever felt truly close to. The woman he'd let call him Daddy. The woman who made his brain melt and his cock hard.

He had to. Because she didn't love him. In fact, she hated him.

And why shouldn't she?

She thought he was greedy. Uncharitable. Cruel to animals.

And even if none of that was entirely true, it hadn't come out of nowhere. She had a point.

He stole a look in the rearview mirror, unable to believe how gorgeous she'd looked in those mint-green overalls. He wished he could stop the car. Talk things through with her. Apologize for being cruel. Swear to her that he wasn't the bad guy she thought he was. That he—

Fuck!

He must have kept his eyes off the road ahead for too long because something large and brown appeared in front of him out of nowhere. An animal.

He slammed on the brakes as hard as he could.

Please don't hit it.

Please.

Just then, he felt something bang into him from behind. No! Peach!

He jumped out the car, running back to her, making sure she was okay. She was open-mouthed and fuming, yelling something at him that he couldn't hear while she was in the car. But seeing her like that was a relief. She looked pissed rather than hurt. Which meant he had something more pressing to attend to.

He ran over to the front of his car and was shocked to see a cow lying on the road in front of it. As far as he could tell, his tires hadn't hit the animal. It was at least a couple yards away. But if that was the case, why was the animal just lying there?

He crouched down to take a closer look. His heart was racing and his breath was shallow, but he stayed as quiet and still as possible so he didn't scare the creature. Moving around to the back of the animal, his eyes widened when he saw what was happening. The cow was giving birth! There was something sticking out of it. Hard to tell what it was, since it was encased in fetal membranes, but it looked like the start of two front feet.

"What's going on?" Peach was right behind him, whispering. "Did you hit it?"

He turned and put his finger to his lips. "Call 911," he whispered back to her. "She's giving birth. We need a vet. Or the farmer. Or both."

Peach took out her phone, and he turned back to the cow.

"It's alright, girl," he said, keeping his distance, staying calm and quiet. He could tell from the tag in the cow's ear that it wasn't one of his aunt's. That was obvious, anyway. His aunt's cattle weren't healthy enough to be giving birth. They were half-starved and riddled with disease, poor things.

As he took in the cow's situation, memories bubbled up in him from a distant past. His father's voice, soothing and kind. "If the presentation is normal, you can let the cow labor for forty minutes to an hour. No more."

He had no way of knowing how long the cow had been in labor, but he was pretty sure it had only recently started. Its breath was steady, it didn't look too exhausted. The water bag was still in place around the calf.

"There's no signal," Peach said, her voice a little raised.

"It's okay," Isaac said calmly. "We don't need to panic." He pulled his phone out of his pocket and saw that he had no signal either. Damn. They were too far away from Aunt Meg's ranch now. He was just going to have to get the delivery done here.

"What should I do?" Peach asked, wringing her hands. "Should I stroke the cow? Try to pull out the calf?"

"No," he said firmly. "She's doing just great like this. She knows what to do. We need to give her space." He paused. "There are some shirts and jackets in the trunk of my car. Get them, would you?"

He tossed the keys to Peach, keeping his eyes on the cow. She was still breathing normally. That was good.

Alright. Time to check the fetus.

He didn't have any surgical gloves, but he always carried a small bottle of alcohol hand rub with him. A lot of businessmen did that these days — all the handshakes and meetings you had to go through in a day. He cleaned his hands, just in case, and then he took the shirts and jackets from Peach and laid them down at the cow's rear. The road was dirty and rough, and his shirts were clean and soft. The perfect landing spot for a calf.

"Wait," said Peach. "Those are designer jackets. They say Gucci on the label. Won't that ruin them?"

Isaac smiled up at her. "Plenty more suits out there. But only one of this little calf."

He examined the part of the sac that he could see, being careful not to get too close to the cow in case she got scared. He could see two hooves. His heart raced. He could hear his father's voice again.

"If the hoof pads are facing upward, son, you have to pull the calf. Don't hesitate."

He looked more closely and saw that the pads were facing downward.

Thank god. He could breathe again.

"Is everything... alright?" Peach whispered.

"It's all good, babygirl," he replied. It took him by surprise that he just called her that, but then this whole situation was taking him by surprise. "Now, listen carefully. I want you to walk to the top of that hill over there, and I want you to try to get a signal. I want you to check the location on GPS and then relay it to emergency services. I think this cow's gonna be just fine, but we need backup."

Peach looked into his eyes, taking in his every word, and then she nodded. "Yes, Daddy. I can do that."

Isaac looked back at the cow and was delighted to see that the contractions had pushed even more of the calf out of it out. Everything looked normal. Healthy. Kind of amazing, actually. As Isaac watched the cow do exactly what nature intended her to do, he became aware of something. The feeling of his father's hand, pressed down on his shoulder, just firmly enough to let him know that he was there.

"Dad?" he whispered, with tears in his eyes.

"I'm here, son," said his father. "And now you're here too. Back where you belong."

Isaac nodded, crying, and then he watched the cow give a deep breath.

The calf plopped out of its mother's body, quickly but gently, and the birth was complete.

Isaac edged farther away, giving the creature space. He watched the mother get to her feet, then she turned to the calf and began licking it clean, letting it know that it was safe and loved. Showing it that it had a place in the world, right here.

"Good girl," he whispered to the cow. "You did great."

"I did?" said Peach, returning, a brave smile on her face. Then she froze, looking at the cow. "Oh my goodness! There's blood all over your shirts! What happened?"

"The calf was born," said Isaac, standing up and putting his arm around Peach. "Everything is good."

Peach gave a huge sigh of relief, and he could see how stressed out the poor girl had been. "I managed to call emergency services. I told them about the green tag in the cow's ear and they knew the farmer. He's on his way out here. I think a vet's coming too."

"You did good, babygirl," he said, squeezing Peach's hand. He felt his father's hand still resting upon his own shoulder, and a great calmness washed over him.

"Isaac?" Peach asked. "Are you okay? You're looking kind of... weird."

"I feel... healed," Isaac replied.

"Healed?"

"By love."

Peach cocked her head at him. "Okay, now I think something's definitely up. You don't sound like Real Isaac to me. Are you a fake?"

Isaac smiled. "Actually, I think I'm more real than I've ever been."

He looked at Peach, really looked at her. His kind, sensitive, sweet wife. So full of big-hearted ambition and love for the universe.

"Peach," he said softly. "I'm ready to start the rest of my life now. And I'm ready to start it with you."

Peach bit her lip, looking off to one side. "I... don't know... We just went through something pretty traumatic. Here, but also at the ranch. And then back in Miami, too. That argument. I just don't know if we're—"

"Let's at least talk," Isaac told her. "There are things I want to tell you. Things I want to explain. At least then you'll know who I really am. And then you can decide how you feel.""So you know how you feel?" Peach asked. "It feels like, just a hot minute ago, you were pretty mad at me. You're not mad anymore?"

"I'm mad as hell," Isaac replied, quick as a whip. "But not at you, Peach Trimble. In fact, asking you to marry me was the sanest thing I ever did."

Chapter Twenty

PEACH

"I'M ONLY HERE BECAUSE I'm worried about you," Peach said. "I wouldn't normally agree to stay in a dirty motel with a man who said marrying me was a waste of time."

The cow had been reunited with the farmer. Apparently, he had a length of broken fencing and the cow had wandered off. A vet had turned up too, and both of them had congratulated Isaac on a job well done. Isaac, who had showered since dealing with the birth of the cow, and was now pacing up and down the small room, turned to her, confused. "I said that?"

"Back in Miami. When you found out your aunt wouldn't sell you the ranch."

Isaac sat on the edge of the bed beside her and put his hand on her arm. "I only meant putting you through the whole marriage pact."

"But... you didn't put me through anything," Peach said with a shrug. "I'd been enjoying myself up to that point."

"Even though you think I'm... how did you put it... a greedy asshole who hates animals and would never give anything to charity?"

Peach blushed. "I don't remember using any of those words, Daddy."

She wasn't sure why that word had slipped out a couple of times. Was Isaac her Daddy anymore? Unlikely after everything that had happened between them. But he had called her "babygirl" a few times, and it felt good when he did. Natural, somehow. It was the same for her calling him Daddy.

"You know what?" said Isaac. "There's some truth in that stuff. I *am* greedy, in the sense that I enjoy making money. Hell, I fucking love it. It's been a hobby of mine since I was a kid, and it turns out I'm really damn good at it."

Peach grimaced. It didn't seem right, somehow, for somebody to admit that they loved money that much.

"But... you love money too, don't you, Peach?" Isaac asked.

"I... well, I had fun going shopping with you. And staying in the mansion. But I also felt kind of guilty keeping everything to myself. So when I thought about setting up a pet rescue center—"

"It felt good to give something back, right?"

"Right."

Isaac nodded. "Of course it did. You don't think that I keep everything I earn, do you? That I don't give to charity?"

Peach scratched her nose, even though it wasn't itchy. "Um. No?"

"I don't normally like to shout about this stuff. Seems a bit... gauche. But I give twenty percent of everything I make to charity. Well, more accurately, I split it between three charities."

"You do?" Peach asked, fidgeting awkwardly. "Which, er, which three charities?"

She was half-hoping that he'd name really shitty charities and she could call him out on it, but when she thought about it, there weren't really any shitty charities.

"I tend to rotate the charities each year, to keep it as fair as possible. This year it's Save the Children, UNICEF, and Defenders of Wildlife."

"Defenders of Wildlife?" asked Peach, remembering what had happened at the shopping mall. The guy that had come up to them asking for money was from the Defenders of Wildlife. "Why did you send that guy away when we were out at the mall? He was from your chosen charity! You didn't need to be so rude to him."

"Honestly, my PA chooses my charities," said Isaac awkwardly. "But also... I happen to think that there's a time and a place for asking people for money. We were just sitting down for a meal. I was pissed, if I'm being honest, at our date being interrupted. I was worried he'd ruin the moment."

"The way you spoke to him was the only thing that ruined the moment," Peach said.

"Point taken," said Isaac. "And... I'm sorry. I should be more considerate. There's a reason that charities need to ask people for money. And people make their donations in all kinds of ways. In public, in private, with their time, with their money." He looked at Peach intently. "I want to be a better man, Peach."

"And what does that mean to you?" Peach asked, confused. "Being a better man?"

"Something has happened to me, Peach," Isaac said. "Well, a lot of things actually. First, we met. And we got married. And being with you has cracked me in two, you know? It's opened me up to all kinds of new things. I feel so vulnerable, for the first time in years."

"I feel that too," Peach said quietly.

"Then, I lost the ranch," Isaac continued. "The land where my parents are buried. The place I still, in my heart, call home."

Peach felt a pang of guilt. To think that she had ever thought she might steal that from him. His rightful home.

"You know what I was thinking as I drove away from the ranch today?" Isaac said. "After my aunt told us to get off her land? I was thinking that I'd lost something huge. That I'd lost *you*."

"You were thinking about me?" Peach asked, her voice suddenly very little.

"That ranch meant everything to me," said Isaac. "But it's in the past now. You, Peach Trimble, are my future."

Peach blinked at him, building up the bravery to speak her truth. "You're a great man, Isaac. A truly brilliant, man. And I love you even more for how honest you're being with me right now. But... I don't know that our dreams align. I still want to set up a rescue center. It made me feel so alive when I came up with the idea. And then there's Teddy, who's sleeping in the car right now and it's easy to forget that he's part of my life, but—"

"I love Teddy," said Isaac, without skipping a beat. "And I love you."

Peach jumped up off the bed, as though her butt had been burned. "You can't say that. Not if you don't mean it."

Isaac grabbed her hand, and pulled her toward him, down onto his lap. "Babygirl," he said, "you have to listen to me. I love your dog. I'm having immunotherapy so I can get close to him without sneezing my ass off. And I love your pet rescue center idea too. In fact, I'm just gonna say it: I love animals. Period."

"You... love... me?" Peach said, her brain trying to catch up. "And you... love... animals?"

Isaac stroked a lick of hair away from her face, tucking it behind her ear. "Yes, darling," he said. "Both of those things are true."

"But... the first time you saw me... in the office with Teddy..."

"I was worked up about my allergies," said Isaac, then he let out a long sigh. "But there's something else." He paused. "My mom and dad both died of poisoning. Naturally-occuring anthrax in the soil, the coroner said, but it was spread to them via the cattle. I was young when they died, and I never forgave the animals for killing them. The day after they died, I started sneezing whenever a cow came near me. Then it was a dog. Then a cat. Then any animal with fur."

Peach put her hand over her mouth. Her eyes filled with tears. "The animals remind you of losing your parents."

"Yes," said Isaac. "Every cough, every sneeze, every itchy eyeball, was a reminder of what I lost. And, I'm ashamed to admit it, I guess I kinda hated animals for it."

"I think I understand," said Peach. "I feel so sad for you. But... is that why you left the ranch? Because you didn't want to be around the cattle?"

"Nope," said Isaac, his jaw hardening. "That was my aunt's doing. She turned up at the ranch the day before the funeral waving a piece of paper in my fourteen-year-old face. Told me that she had a will, and that it said that the ranch was to be left to her."

"Do you think the will was real?"

"I do," Isaac replied, "but I think there must have been a more recent copy. My father always used to tell me that the ranch would be mine one day. He was training me up to take it over. I think my aunt destroyed that will, but I never had proof."

There were tears running down Peach's cheeks now. "Oh, Isaac. You've been through so much. I was going to buy the ranch for you, you know? I was going to give it to you. I'm so sorry that we've lost it now."

"No," said Isaac. "Don't be sorry. If there's a chance that I haven't lost you, then I'm still the luckiest man alive."

Peach laughed as she sobbed, and Isaac wiped the tears from his cheek with his thumb.

Then, he kissed her.

It was the most tender, most honest, most beautiful kiss of her life. Not the kiss of a Daddy. Not right now. It was the kiss of a husband.

But as the kiss grew more passionate, and Peach's pussy started to throb and grow wet, she felt the kiss change. *Now* it was the kiss of a Daddy. A Daddy who wanted to heal things between them as only a Daddy knew how.

"This is me, babygirl," panted Isaac between kisses. "The real me. The me who wants to hold you, to have you." He bit down on her earlobe, making her gasp. "When we saw that creature out there today, I realized that what you said was true."

"Wh-what?" asked Peach, dizzy with lust. "What did I say?"

"You said that we're all animals. And you're right. We're just creatures, bristling with instincts and needs, hunger and passion." He unhooked one strap of her overalls and slid his finger inside her t-shirt, squeezing her breast. "I'm a *beast*, Peach Trimble. I can't pretend I'm not any longer. I'm a filthy, fucking beast. And I want to do filthy, fucking things to you, you little animal."

Peach gasped as Isaac lifted her off him and threw her face-down on the bed. "In this grubby motel?" she asked, looking back at him, still panting. "It doesn't really seem like your style, Daddy."

"*You're* my style, Peach," he said. "Putting my cock in you, wherever and whenever, is just how I like it."

He pulled down her overalls, then took down his own pants. She couldn't believe how hard he was already. And how wet she was.

"Um... that's... the kind of style I can get behind..." She was saying goofy things because she suddenly felt nervous. The things that were happening between them felt so much more real now. No fakery. No pretense. Just his naked body and her naked body, together in this hotel.

"Speaking of behind," said Isaac, climbing onto the bed behind her and lifting her by the hips. "Get that butt in the air for me, Mrs. Righton."

Peach got onto all fours, lifting her ass high up in the air.

"Good," said Isaac. "Very good."

She looked down between her legs and saw him kneeling behind her, stroking his cock. How was he about to take her? In her ass? In her pussy? Both?

"You have no idea," said Isaac, his voice shaky, "how often I fantasize about this thick ass." He took hold of her round cheeks and began massaging them.

She'd always felt self-conscious of her wobbly bum. Her pear-shaped figure. The way her flesh sat around her middle. But the way Isaac touched her made her feel like the most beautiful woman alive.

"This soft belly," said Isaac, sliding his fingers up to her tummy now, rubbing and stroking her like she was his little pet. "Mmmm. I just wanna get my face in there."

She felt his breath on her ass now, and then, out of nowhere, she felt a tongue on her butthole.

Holy heck!

Was that okay? Was it alright that he was licking her bum? Did it taste okay? Did it feel good for him?

She needn't have worried. As Isaac ate her butt, his face buried deep between her cheeks, he made the kind of noises that told Peach that he was finding the whole experience utterly delicious. He massaged her tummy as his tongue probed her back passage, and she found herself grinding her hips back into him, pushing his tongue in deeper and deeper.

"Oh, Daddy..." she murmured. "I feel like I need to touch myself..."

Her hand trailed toward her trickling wet pussy, but Daddy took firm hold of it and moved it away.

She wriggled and squirmed and bucked, but Daddy didn't give in. He kept his tongue inside her ass and let her pussy ache in desperation. The tip of his tongue was pushing some secret part of her, tickling some sensitive area that drove her pussy wild with desire.

"I need... I need..." she gasped.

Her pussy had never felt more hungry, more desperate to be filled. But Isaac seemed intent on teasing her. Was it possible that she could come like this? She certainly felt close. As if she was perpetually on the edge. If she could just touch her clit for one tiny second, she knew that she'd come in an instant.

"Mmmmm...." she moaned, low and guttural. "I think... I... thn-nnnfffff...." Words eluded her now. She was in animal mode.

And so was he. Licking and grunting and moaning with pleasure as he ate her butt. But then, suddenly, he pulled away, and she felt the soft, warm tip of his dick nudging her butthole.

"I'm gonna fuck you in the ass now, babygirl," he told her. "Hold on tight, my little animal."

Her asshole was nice and wet for him, and his cock stretched her open with ease.

"No pussy-fucking for you today, little one," he panted as he fucked her. "This is your punishment for trying to buy Daddy's ranch. Naughty... little... creature..." He panted as he thrust mercilessly into her.

Her whole body shook. Her large breasts swung back and forth. Her tummy wobbled and her ass jiggled. Her pussy stayed on the edge of that orgasm constantly.

"Fuck," Isaac panted, "I'm gonna come in your ass, little animal."

She felt him stretch her open even more now, and then he throbbed inside of her, the hot liquid pouring out of him and into her center.

Ho-lee shit.

She shook and spasmed and trembled, so, so, so close to coming.

"Daddy, please!" she whined. "I'm begging you!"

Isaac grabbed hold of her dangling breast with one hand, and then she felt his middle finger sink deep into her wet, open pussy.

As he skewered her on his long, thick finger, he yanked her by the hair, pulling her back as far as she would go, getting his finger in as deep as possible. His cock was still hard and deep in her ass.

"Come on my finger," he growled. "On finger is all you're allowed, babygirl."

Peach had never done this before. Never come so hard and force-fully with just one finger inside her, completely still. But now, she felt the tidal wave surge inside her and she shuddered and clenched and tightened around Daddy's middle finger like it was her entire world.

And then... peace.

*

Another shower, this time for both of them. Isaac had rubbed soap all over her, and he'd gotten so hard touching her body that she thought he was going to fuck her again. She *hoped* he would.

"Are you still mad at me, Daddy?" asked Peach as they lay naked under the thin, unappealing blankets at the hotel. "You know I would never have taken your ranch away from you, don't you?"

Isaac smiled. "I know, babygirl. You're a sweet, kind thing. There's not a single bad bone in your body."

"Speaking of bones," said Peach, "I should probably take Teddy out for a walk soon."

Teddy was sleeping on the floor in his basket. Peach didn't like to wake him, but she knew he'd want to poop in the night if he didn't go out soon.

"You know what?" said Isaac. "Let me do it. I don't want my Little girl wandering around out there at this time."

"You'd do that?" asked Peach. "You'd walk Teddy all by yourself?"

Isaac laughed. "I'm sure I can manage. Besides, me and the mutt could do with a little time to get to know one another."

"He doesn't really like to be called a mutt," said Peach, giving a mock pout. As she stroked Isaac's arm, she noticed something. A long pink scratch running down his forearm. "Hey, I didn't do that, did I? I'm sorry if it was me!"

Isaac looked at the scratch and then back at Peach. "Ah. No. That wasn't you. That was... Okay, there's something you don't know about me yet."

Peach sat up in the bed, frowning. "There is? What is it? You... get random scratches on your arm that you can't explain?"

"No," said Isaac. "That's not it. I *can* explain the scratch. Only... you're gonna find the reason a bit... surprising."

"I am?"

"I... have a cat," said Isaac.

"You have a *what*?"

"It was never meant to be permanent. It's a stray kitten. Turned up on my doorstep a couple weeks ago. I've been trying to re-home it, but..."

Peach giggled. "You've grown attached to it, haven't you?"

Isaac looked deep into Peach's eyes, suddenly serious. He put his arm around her, pulling her in close. "I want a family, Peach. I never knew it until now. I always felt scared to have one, in case I lost it like

I lost my mom and dad. But... I want you. And I want Teddy. And I want Itchy."

"Itchy?" Peach asked, screwing up her nose.

"Yep. That's the kitten's name. Guess Itchy's kind of a silly name now that I'm getting immunotherapy. She won't be making me itchy for much longer."

"It's a cute name," said Peach. "And... I want a family too."

Since seeing that cow give birth, something had been percolating in her mind. Brewing and getting stronger. She'd been afraid to say anything at first, in case she was wrong. In case Isaac was too mad at her to listen.

But now, the idea felt so right. And the vision she had in her head felt so wonderful that she had to share it.

"Daddy," she said, "I have a plan."

Chapter Twenty-One

ISAAC

THIS WAS THE CRAZIEST thing he'd ever done. But if it worked... Peach Trimble was a damn genius.

"Any sign of danger and you run back to your car, babygirl," said Isaac. "I'll follow right behind you."

Peach nodded, smiling. "It'll be fine, Daddy. I promise."

They had parked a little way back from the ranch and they were hiding behind a tree. Peach looked adorable. Her eyes were shining brighter than ever before, and he was so damn in love with her, it was ridiculous.

They'd spent the night at the motel, formulating their plan. Isaac had taken Teddy for a walk and he'd brought Peach breakfast in bed this morning: croissants and fruit and juice. The one thing he hadn't done, which he was desperate to do, was fuck her again. But he knew that Peach was enjoying being made to wait. He knew that when he finally entered her pussy again, it would be explosive.

"You got your phone, Daddy?" Peach asked.

"Yup," said Isaac, holding it up. "You got yours?"

"Yes!" Peach said, holding up hers too.

"Then we're good to go, babygirl. Let's do this thing." He bent down and kissed Peach on the cheek. He would have kissed her on the lips but he didn't trust himself not to get carried away. Enacting this plan with her was so exciting that it was kind of a turn-on. Even if it didn't work, it was hot as hell that she was willing to do this for him. He just hoped that she'd play it safe.

Peach clapped her hands together and jumped up and down. She was wearing a pink PAW patrol t-shirt and her breasts jiggled temptingly as she moved. "Come on, Teddy!" she squealed. "Pups to the rescue!"

She began skipping up to the ranch house with Teddy in tow, and Isaac watched her with bated breath.

Finally, after what felt like an eternity, Peach reached the door of the ranch house. Isaac saw her knock on the door, then get her phone out her pocket as planned. The moment that Aunt Meg opened the door, Peach pressed a button on her phone, and Teddy started running around and yapping like all hell had broken loose.

"What's going on?" Isaac heard Aunt Meg cry. "Get that dog under control!"

But Peach couldn't control Teddy, because she had started to play the PAW Patrol theme tune on her phone, and apparently, whenever she did that, Teddy became extremely hyper. In fact, he was so overexcited that he ran right into the ranch house, as Peach predicted that he would.

"I'm so sorry!" Peach exclaimed.

And without skipping a beat, Aunt Meg ran into the house after the dog.

Peach turned and gave Isaac a thumbs up, then she went into the house after Aunt Meg.

Now was Isaac's chance. He headed straight for the cattle, taking photographs of their half-starved bodies and their terrible living conditions. It was nerve-wracking wondering how Peach was getting on inside the house, and he knew that he had to work quickly. When he had a dozen or so pictures, he stopped. That would be enough.

But there was one more thing he wanted to do before he left. There was a chance that the plan might not work, and if it didn't... he wanted to see his parents' graves one last time.

He ran from tree to tree, trying to blend in, until he reached the back of the ranch house. And the moment that he saw his mom and dad's graves, he felt the bile rising in his stomach. What a mess. Aunt Meg had treated them with total disrespect. They were full of weeds and trash. It was hard to look.

"Mom," he said sorrowfully, "Dad. I'm sorry. I'm gonna make this right."

He knew, there and then, that no matter what happened, he was going to get this ranch back. And when he did, he wasn't going to make this place into any kind of investment. He was going to make it into a home.

Just then, he heard a scream inside the ranch house. He looked through the back window and saw Aunt Meg holding up a rolling pin, trying to batter Teddy with it.

"No!" Peach screamed. "Stop!"

He ran over to the house and knocked on the window. "Aunt Meg!" he yelled. "I'm the one you ought to come after! Because I'm the one that's about to get this whole place shut down!"

Aunt Meg ran over to the window, and, without thinking, she bashed it with the rolling pin, smashing the glass.

"You piece of shit, Isaac!" she yelled. "Just like your father! Trying to take something that doesn't belong to him!"

Isaac looked at her squarely. "What are you talking about?"

Aunt Meg paused for breath. Then, she wheezed: "Your father, my brother. He wanted my Jeffrey's land. Before he died."

Isaac looked at her through the broken glass. Her face looked twisted up by years of bitterness.

"Uncle Jeffrey used to own the pastureland next to this one," said Isaac. "But... the land was no good. Nothing would grow on it. And the animals kept dying."

"The land," said Aunt Meg, screwing her eyes tight shut, "had anthrax on it. But Jeffrey and I were dealing with it."

"Wait," said Isaac, his head reeling, "so why did my father want the land? Did he know about the anthrax?"

Aunt Meg hung her head. "No. Your father didn't know. He just wanted to expand his ranch. Said we were making a meal of the land and offered to buy us out for a pittance."

"You can't blame my father for wanting to expand the ranch, can you?" Isaac asked.

"Your father," said Aunt Meg, with gritted teeth, "was greedy. Just like you. You know what he did? When Jeffrey wouldn't sell him the land, he called animal control. Got Jeffrey into trouble. Jeffrey was forced to give up the land, and your dad bought it for peanuts."

"I remember dad buying that land," said Isaac, trying to piece this together. "That was about a year before he died." Just then, it hit him like a freight train. "Wait. So Uncle Jeffrey's land had anthrax on it? And my father's didn't?"

Aunt Meg scratched her cheek furiously. "He asked me to put some of the soil on your dad's land. I didn't know it would... I didn't realize that your parents..."

Isaac's blood began to boil. "You're responsible for their deaths?"

"It was Jeffrey's idea," said Aunt Meg, her voice starting to waver. "And he was the one who destroyed the will. I just..." She dropped the rolling pin, and bent-double, crying. Then, she looked up at Isaac, her eyes narrow and mean. "It's been a great burden to live with this, Isaac. But you know what? You've hardly suffered. In fact, you made money out of this. You left the countryside and made your fortune in Miami. Everything you have, all of it, is because of what I did." She folded her arms. "So now you know the truth. Maybe you and your weirdo wife will get off my property and stop bothering me. Because you're both just as bad as me. And I'll deny what I just told you until the day I die."

There was a noise behind Aunt Meg, and Peach stepped forward, holding her phone high. "I can stop recording now, Daddy, can't I?" she said. "I think we got more than we ever bargained for."

Aunt Meg turned around and looked at Peach. "You were filming this, you little freak? Give that here!" As the old woman lurched forward, Isaac yelled at Peach to get out.

And that is exactly what she did, with Teddy running close behind her.

Isaac ran around the side of the house to meet her, and the three of them didn't stop running until they were back at the cars.

"Daddy," Peach said, looking up at him, "I'm so sorry. All those things she said."

Isaac took her head in her hands. "Darling," he said, "I'm so glad that you're..." But try as he might, he couldn't get the words out. He was crying. He was holding her. He was kissing her. He was ready to make everything right.

Chapter Twenty-Two

PEACH

"You know, I never would have had you down as a zoo kind of a guy," said Peach, grinning, as she licked her mint choc chip ice-cream.

"You kidding? This was my favorite place when I was a kid," said Isaac. "We used to come to Miami just to visit the zoo when I was a kid... before... well, you know."

Peach squeezed Isaac's hand. "You sure you don't want a lick of my ice-cream, Daddy?"

Isaac looked at the ice-cream. "Careful," he said, "or you'll make Daddy hard in public yet again. I'll never forget that strawberry ice-cream incident."

Peach fluttered her lashes at him. "What strawberry ice-cream incident, Daddy? Explain it to me."

"Bad girl," he growled, squeezing her bottom, quickly enough that it was barely noticeable to anyone else here, but hard enough that Peach *definitely* noticed it.

As they walked past cute animal after cute animal, Peach let out a happy sigh. "I don't know what I like best: mammals or reptiles."

Isaac laughed. "It's a real conundrum. Mammals are normally a lot cuddlier-looking than reptiles. But reptiles are badass, so..."

"It's like the difference between you and me, Daddy," Peach joked.

The winter sun shone down on them, and everything felt so good. Yesterday, they'd come back from the ranch after dropping in at a police station with all the evidence they'd amassed. Isaac told Peach, as they came away from it, that it felt like a weight had been lifted from his shoulders. Finally finding out the truth. Seeing his aunt confess.

The police said that they'd be firm but fair with Aunt Meg. If she cooperated with them, and if what she was saying was true, it was Jeffrey who had been the brains behind the operation. It had all happened years ago, and would be hard to prove, but Aunt Meg wasn't going to get away without jail time. What she had done was manslaughter at the very best. And being involved in the destruction of a will — that was fraud. Throw in the animal neglect, and Aunt Meg's situation wasn't exactly rosy.

Still, she deserved whatever she had coming, that was for sure. The cops had told Isaac that it might take a little time to sort everything out, but that he had a good chance of getting the ranch taken away from his aunt, and restored to him, the rightful owner.

Peach felt amazing to have played a part in all that. Helping other people was one of her hobbies, after all. They still hadn't talked about what Isaac would do with the ranch, if he got it back, but that would come.

"What you thinking about, babygirl?" he asked as they stopped by a cage of giant anteaters.

Peach took a deep breath. "The future."

Isaac looked at her thoughtfully. "You know, we can't annul our marriage anymore... Not since we... But of course, we can divorce any time you like..." He put his arms around her waist. "It's not what I want, though."

"What do you want?" asked Peach, her voice small and tremulous.

"I want to take back the ranch," said Isaac.

Peach's heart sank. He was thinking about the ranch, not about her. Of course, the ranch was a big deal for him, but she'd hoped that he—

"And I want to set up your animal rescue center on it."

Peach's eyes widened. "You do?"

"Except, I think, I want it to be a home. For me, and you, and all of the animals who live there."

Peach swallowed. "You mean... like... a sanctuary?"

"Exactly," said Isaac. "I want to help rescue badly treated animals and look after them on our sanctuary. I know it's not exactly the same as a pet rescue center, but I want the ranch to be a home, and—"

"I love it," Peach said quickly. "It's perfect."

"We have space for at least a couple hundred cattle on that land," Isaac continued, the words flowing out of him excitedly, "plus a bunch of other creatures. And there'll be Teddy and Itchy, of course, plus me and you..." He moved his palm around to Peach's tummy. "Plus, if it appeals to you, a dozen or so tiny little Peaches?"

"A dozen!" Peach gasped. "You want twelve kids?"

"Okay, maybe six," joked Isaac. "Only if it's what you want, that is—"

"Yes, Daddy," said Peach quickly, "I do. I do!"

Isaac laughed, lifting her into the air and twirling her around.

"Careful, Daddy! I'm heavy!" Peach said, giggling.

"Nonsense," Isaac said, putting her down. "Wait until you're pregnant with these half dozen children, darling. Then you'll know what heavy is."

"I hope I don't have to be pregnant with them all at once!" Peach said, blushing.

"It's not a deal-breaker," Isaac replied, stooping down and taking a lick of her ice-cream.

"Hey, get your own, meanie!" Peach said, pouting, but she was only joking. Her Daddy could lick anything of hers he liked.

They walked on a little way, past small-clawed otters, giant elands, and meerkats. Isaac seemed deep in thought.

"While we wait to set up the ranch," he said, "I'd like to work on another project."

"Oh yes?" asked Peach.

"The honeymoon mansion. The one we argued in before we came out here. It's actually always kinda been my favorite. It's in the best position for the ocean view. It just needs doing up."

"I'd love to do it up," Peach said.

"I'd like to make it into a home with you. Combining both our tastes."

Peach snickered. "You mean, contemporary billionaire meets cartoon-loving Little?"

"Exactly," Isaac replied sincerely. "That's exactly how it should be. And then, when we're done, I'd like to sell the other three mansions on the compound. I don't need them all, you know. And I'd like to put half the money I make from it toward setting up the sanctuary."

"What about the other half?" Peach asked. "Some kind of investment?"

"Nope," Isaac replied. "I want you to choose which charities to donate it to. I figured you might find it fun."

"I would find it fun!" Peach replied, glowing. "Super fun!"

"Good," Isaac said, kissing her. "Then it's settled. I love you, Mrs. Righton."

"I love you, Daddy Righton."

Isaac kissed Peach's cheek, then whispered into her ear: "There's a meerkat behind you."

Peach jumped, then squealed, then laughed. Then, suddenly, her gaze dropped to the floor.

"What is it, darling?" Isaac asked. "What's up?"

"It's nothing," Peach sniffed. "It's... I'm so happy... I just wish my friends..."

Isaac put his hand over her beating heart. "I think we can fix this."

Chapter
Twenty-Three

ISAAC

WHO SAID YOU COULDN'T take your friends on your honey-moon? There was plenty of room on this boat for all of them. It wasn't the enormous luxury cruise liner that he'd booked for him and Peach, but it was a very nice yacht with three double cabins and a pool. And there was nothing like cruising between some of Europe's most historic tourist spots to remind everyone why they were all still friends.

"Oh man, I needed this," said Kiera, stretching out on the deck.

Isaac, who was sorting drinks for everyone, couldn't help notice the way that Bastion was staring at her. The two of them had barely said a word to each other, but they seemed to look at each other constantly. They either wanted to fight or fuck, he couldn't figure it out.

"Tell me about it," said Daisy, lying on a lounger beside her. "Thanks for letting us come on your honeymoon, Peachy Pop."

Peach was in the pool, throwing a beach ball up and down. She looked incredible in her little pink bikini, all her curves on display, reminding Isaac of what a lucky guy he was. She wasn't showing yet, though, which was just as well, because it seemed a little bit soon to tell everyone about that. Six weeks pregnant, though. It was a great feeling. All this time, and all this money, and what he'd really needed had been a beautiful wife and a wonderful family.

"When are you guys gonna play with meeeee?" Peach called to Daisy and Kiera.

Daisy looked over at her with a wicked grin. "Aren't you going to say: '*Ziiiiiiip*?'" She said that last bit in a high-pitched voice that made everyone look at her in bemusement.

Peach clapped her hands excitedly. "*Ziiip! Ziiiip! Ziiiiiiip!*"

"Is someone going to tell me what's happening here?" asked Isaac.

"They're speaking Gigglish," Kiera told him. "It's a secret language they made up years ago."

Out of nowhere, Daisy began to snort like a pig.

Peach shook her head and snorted like a pig in return.

"I believe they're saying 'Thank you' to each other," Kiera translated for the group.

Everyone cracked up. It was so good to see the girls getting on like this. Kiera and Daisy seemed genuinely happy for Peach and Isaac now, and it was like they'd never been apart. Obviously, getting them back on side had taken time and patience. Isaac had apologized to Kiera and Daisy for not earning their trust properly. And Kiera and Daisy had apologized to Peach for not trusting her more in the first place.

The poor girls had promised not to fall out ever again. To always trust each other no matter what, and to be best friends forever. They all seemed to have learned something from the experience, and that was heartwarming to see.

Daisy raised her hands. "Alright, alright, I'm getting in! I was going to play with my new Beach Barbie set that Daddy got me, but I guess it can wait..."

Montague walked over to Daisy and kissed the top of her head. Then, he lifted her high into the air, making Daisy scream, and threw her into the pool.

"Naughty Daddy!" Daisy shouted, splashing water at him. "That was very, very bad!"

Montague laughed. "Guess I'll have to suffer the same punishment then," he said, jumping into the pool, fully clothed.

"Hey, wait for me!" squealed Kiera, jumping into the pool in her shorts and t-shirt.

It was great to see everyone goofing around like this. Even Bastion was laughing, and he'd barely smiled since his divorce. Life was good. Friends and family were everything.

"Come on, Daddy!" Peach laughed. "You have to get in too! Last one in's a rotten egg!"

Isaac looked at Bastion. "Looks like we're in this together, dude."

Bastion didn't even wait to be invited. He did a running jump, cannonballing into the end of the pool, splashing everyone and causing screams and laughter among the Littles.

"Uh oh," said Peach. "Looks like you're the rotten egg, Daddy."

"It's true," said Isaac. "You got me." He pretended to take a huge gulp of the sangria he'd been mixing, but then he put the glass down and ran over to the pool, jumping in with the force of a man who was never going to hold back, ever again.

"This is the life," said Peach, swimming over to him.

"It sure is," said Daisy. "Hey, Peach. I'm sorry for being judgy and... kind of a Bridezilla about your wedding. I'm glad you're with Isaac."

"Yeah," said Kiera, looking straight into Isaac's eyes. "He's not so bad, after all. But if he hurts you, I *will* kill him."

"That's fair enough," said Isaac, laughing. "I fully accept my fate."

Isaac wasn't sure if Peach had told her friends that they'd married for money yet, but it didn't really seem to matter. The truth was that whatever reason they'd married for, they were staying married because they loved one another.

And Isaac was going to look after his wife, his Little, his love, for the rest of her life.

Chapter Twenty-Four

PEACH

Dirt. Poop. Barks. Bleating. Mooing. The perfect chaos of their perfect home.

"Daddy," said Peach, crawling around the floor of the almost finished luxury ranch house, "am I allowed to stop my punishment now?"

"No," said Isaac. He was sitting on an armchair by the fire, with Itchy the cat sleeping on his lap, and Teddy sleeping at his feet.

Itchy and Teddy weren't their only pets now, though. There was Woody the three-legged German Shepherd, Billy the blind bulldog, and Bandit the Jack Russell with PTSD. All Peach's favorite dogs from the rescue center back in Connecticut. She'd felt so sad about quitting on them completely, and when Isaac had asked what was up, the second she'd explained he told her to fly them over. *The more the merrier*, he'd said.

Peach couldn't believe how much he'd changed since that first time they'd met. The animal-hating businessman, who hated to see even one thing out of place, had become completely at peace in the countryside, with creatures and chaos all around him... and a Little wife who he had dressed up as a naughty fox.

"But Daddy," Peach whined, "I only took *one* cookie without asking."

"You know Daddy's in charge of the cookie jar," Isaac told her, not looking up from his newspaper.

"But I was hungry! You know how I get now I'm pregnant!"

Isaac looked down at her, stifling a smile.

Peach felt very silly, crawling around on her hands and knees, her tummy bulging beneath her. She was only three months pregnant, but they'd had their first scan a couple weeks ago, and they had confirmed that she was pregnant with triplets. Peach had been terrified, but Isaac had told her that he was the happiest man on the planet.

"Only three more until we get to our half dozen," he'd joked to her afterward.

Peach crawled over to Isaac, waggling her ass at him. "This is making me super horny."

Isaac had put a butt plug in her, but it wasn't just any butt plug. It was a butt plug with a big, bushy fox's tail hanging down from it. It swished between her legs as she crawled, making her thighs tickle. Her pussy, like the rest of her body, was bare, except for a headband with fox's ears attached to it.

Isaac put down his paper. "Such a cunning little fox, aren't you?" he said. "Sneaking an extra cookie and then trying to get Daddy to fuck you when you're meant to be having a punishment." He looked at his watch. "But... I guess you've been wearing your costume for nearly two hours now, and we do have plenty of jobs to be getting on with out there."

He pointed out the window, at the poopy, barky, bleaty, perfectly wonderful sanctuary that they were building into their forever home.

Since they'd been living here, Isaac had started wearing jeans and flannel, and he always had this relaxed look on his face that made her heart melt.

Well, he almost always had this relaxed look on his face. Except at times like this. When his eyes narrowed... and his cock hardened.

"Crawl over to that rug, foxy."

Peach did as she was told. She could feel Isaac's eyes on her, and she made sure she put on a show for him, jiggling her ass around just the way he liked it.

"Spread your legs a little wider for Daddy," he said.

She did so, and she heard him walking over to her.

"Good," he said. "Now I want to hear you telling me what a naughty girl you've been."

"I've been a very naughty girl, Daddy," she repeated.

"That the only thing you're allowed in your mouth between now and dinner time is Daddy's hard cock."

"Er, the only thing I'm allowed to eat until dinner is Daddy's cock," she said shyly.

Isaac moved around in front of her. He'd taken off his jeans and underpants, and his flannel shirt was open, showing off his tight, muscular abs. His cock, as predicted, was rock hard.

"Go on, then, foxy," he urged her. "Eat Daddy's cock."

Peach strained her neck upward, then opened wide and took her Daddy's large, throbbing cock between her lips. It tasted even better than the cookie she'd stolen earlier, and she sucked at it hungrily.

"Good little fox," said Isaac, stroking her hair. "Daddy's trained you well."

Peach sucked harder, flicking her tongue across the tip just how Daddy liked it, but Isaac stopped her.

"Fuck, babygirl," he said. "Seeing you crawl around in that thing for the past two hours... Daddy's fit to burst. We're gonna have to take it slower or Daddy's gonna cum right away."

He turned her around so that he was facing her butt now.

"I love your tail, babygirl," he said, applying a little pressure to the butt plug, stretching her ass even wider open. He'd been working on increasing the size of the plugs lately. She couldn't believe how wide her Daddy was able to stretch her, and how hungry it made her pussy when he did it.

She whimpered, dizzy with lust.

"Don't worry, darling," Isaac said, putting his hand between her thighs and gently stroking her clit. "Daddy's punished you enough today. It's time to give you a nice big tasty treat."

He pressed his cock against the entrance to her pussy. She could barely handle it. The butt plug was stretching her so wide that everything felt super sensitive.

And then he squeezed into her. She was tighter than usual because of the space the plug was taking up in her back passage.

"Ooh, I like that," said Isaac. "Such a tight little foxy, aren't you?"

"Yes, Daddy," Peach panted. "But I think I can fit you in."

"Good girl," said Isaac, sliding all the way in, getting nice and deep and snug. When he was in as far as he could get, he smacked her ass, making her jump with surprise, ripples of delicious pain radiating around her buttocks.

"Did I do something wrong, Daddy?" she asked, trying not to let him know she was smiling.

"No, babygirl," Isaac replied. "I just know you like it when I smack your ass while I'm inside you."

"It's true," she said. "I *do* like it."

"You're a naughty little creature," he replied. "You know that, foxy?"

"I know, sir," she panted. "And you're a filthy animal, Daddy."

Isaac smacked her again, harder this time, and it brought such a deep rush of pleasure to her pussy and asshole that she surprised herself by coming on his cock in one abrupt, intense, earth-shattering climax. When she had finished gasping, Isaac began slowly sliding in and out of her.

"Well, that was unexpected," he said, "but very, very good."

"I guess being a naughty girl has its perks," said Peach.

Isaac fucked her harder now, and Peach lost track of the noises she was hearing. The grunts and moans of her Daddy. The whinnies and moos of the horses and cattle outside. She was surrounded by animals, surrounded by love, happier and more fulfilled than she ever thought possible.

"You good, babygirl?" Isaac panted as he built toward his climax. "You ready for Daddy to come inside you?"

"Yes, Daddy," she said, grinning. "Yes, yes, yes."

With that, she felt her Daddy come inside her, hard and hot and more real than life itself.

***

Thanks for reading! I had so much fun writing this one. All that anal play! All that chemistry! I love writing a curvy main character too. And the addition of those animal outfits added a little extra kink. Please take the time to leave a review and let people know your thoughts. I appreciate reviews so much!

If you can't get enough Peach and Isaac, check out this little bonus epilogue for YES DADDY. It'll show you how life on the ranch pans out!

And don't forget to check out the third and final novel in the trilogy, MORE DADDY. It's Kiera and Bastion's story, and it has all the fireworks and feistiness you'd expect from these two!

Don't forget to find me on Facebook and join my newsletter for updates on new releases.

Read on for a full list of all my books.

Love and hugs!

Lucky Moon x o x

Also By Lucky Moon

DADDY SAVES CHRISTMAS (IN A LITTLE COUNTRY CHRISTMAS)

SECOND CHANCE DADDIES

DADDY'S GAME

THE DADDY CONTEST

DADDY'S ORDERS

DRIFTERS MC

DADDY DEMANDS

DADDY COMMANDS

DADDY DEFENDS

DADDIES INC

BOSS DADDY

YES DADDY

COLORADO DADDIES

HER WILD COLORADO DADDY

FIERCE DADDIES

THE DADDIES MC SERIES

DANE

ROCK

HAWK

DADDIES MOUNTAIN RESCUE

MISTER PROTECTIVE

MISTER DEMANDING

MISTER RELENTLESS

SUGAR DADDY CLUB SERIES

PLATINUM DADDY

CELEBRITY DADDY

DIAMOND DADDY

CHAMPAGNE DADDY

LITTLE RANCH SERIES

DADDY'S FOREVER GIRL

DADDY'S SWEET GIRL

DADDY'S PERFECT GIRL

DADDY'S DARLING GIRL

DADDY'S REBEL GIRL

MOUNTAIN DADDIES SERIES

TRAPPED WITH DADDY

LOST WITH DADDY

SAVED BY DADDY

STUCK WITH DADDY

TRAINED BY DADDY

GUARDED BY DADDY

STANDALONE NOVELS

PLEASE DADDY

DDLG MATCHMAKER SERIES

Copyright

Content copyright © Lucky Moon. All rights reserved. First published in 2023.

This book may not be reproduced or used in any manner without the express written permission of the copyright holder, except for brief quotations used in reviews or promotions. This book is licensed for your personal use only. Thanks!

Disclaimer: This is a work of fiction. Names, characters, businesses, places, events, locales, and incidents are either the products of the author's imagination or used in a fictitious manner. Any resemblance to actual persons, living or dead, or actual events is purely coincidental.

Cover Image © ksi, Adobestock.com. Cover Design, Lucky Moon.

Printed in Great Britain
by Amazon

22393304R00115